T
By ...y Incollingo

Copyright, 1995
A Reunion Series Book

Published by Reunion Books
3949 Old SR 446
Bloomington, IN 47401

Cover Design & Illustrations By
Gerald "Mouse" Strange

Other Books By Larry Incollingo
Laughing All The Way
G'bye My Honey
Precious Rascal
Ol' Sam Payton
ECHOES of Journeys Past

See order coupon in back of book to
obtain or reserve books.

SEND A GIFT COPY TO A FRIEND.

ACKNOWLEDGEMENT

For their patience, cooperation, care and dedication in the preparation of this book for press I am grateful to the employees of the *Spencer Evening World* and especially to Terry Schooling and Tonya Fender. LInc.

Happy New Year
Lena S. Bird
from
Cliff Bird & wife

This Book Is Dedicated To The Memory Of
CHRISTINA DiSANDRO INCOLLINGO
My Mother

Perry 11·3·96

"It is the writer's privilege to help man endure by lifting his heart." – William Faulkner

Speech upon receiving the Nobel Prize for Literature.

(December 10, 1950)

TIN CAN MAN
By Larry Incollingo

CONTENTS

AUTHOR'S NOTE

There appeared in a Bedford *Times-Mail* tabloid insert one day a feature story by freelancer Claude Parsons about Orange County octogenarian Clifford S. Bird. In the story Mr. Bird (whom close friends sometimes called "CatBird" because of his love for cats) was quoted as saying his two favorite authors were Louis Lamour and Larry Incollingo.

That was compliment enough. However, the entire front page of the tabloid was a color photograph of Mr. Bird holding side by side a copy of one of Lamour's novels and a copy of my own *G'bye My Honey,* the covers of which were easily legible. Of course I was flattered, not to mention grateful to both my colleague, Mr. Parsons, and my reader, Mr. Bird. Sales of *G'bye My Honey* increased so that a second printing of the book was ordered.

By this time my book *Precious Rascal* was also available and I sent an autographed copy to Mr. Bird. One story in that book, "Goin' Fishin'," amused him so that he wrote me a letter about it. I replied, extending my thanks, and there followed a semblance of correspondence between us. He referred to his writings as "Twitterings" from an "Old Buzzer."

Because his letters about his own past life seemed always to fit the mold of people and places about whom I had written, and because they also parallelled comments I had received over the years from other readers, I elected to excerpt the following from one of them, and a poem by Mr. Bird, to introduce the reader to this book.

"Long Sunday Ending," the letter begins.

"Hello LInc: Writing and reading are the way I kill time while my big fat, snow-white and deaf companion Kitty Billy sleeps. He is great and loving company. I just envy his ability to sleep so much.

"Your stories are about people and places like those I knew in my young days, so reading them is like reliving the past of my youth. As in your books, most of the old timers and villages that I knew are non-existent, or almost so now.

"The first three stanzas of the poem I am inflicting on you barely touch on my life when I was reared by grandparents on a hundred acre, one horse, one cow, hogs and chicken farm. It was surrounded by abandoned fields and the wreckage of a house now and then of old settlers who had worn out the soil, moved on or died."

YOU CAN'T GO BACK

"You can't go back," someone has said.
"You can't go back, the past is dead."
But I go back a long, long way,
To a better time, a happier day.

Back to a boy roaming woods and fields,
Searching for treasures they might yield,
Protected by a dog shaggy and strong,
Wherever I'd go he went along.

Back to the day of cornbread and beans,
Making our living by make-do means.
Our home was a house of hand-hewn logs,
Our food was from chickens, a garden and hogs.

I've traveled many of this world's byways,
Knew danger, pleasure, both good and bad days.
And I relive the past, it isn't dead,
It's very alive in this old head.

Fifty-seven years with a wonderful mate,
But now she's away in a helpless state.
I can see no future for us ahead,
So it's back to the past via this old head.

This poem by Mr. Bird which was written February 22, 1990, is something that I wish I might have written. It reveals in a richness of verse how I feel about the past, that it is not dead that it can be revisited, and relived again and again, in recollective musings, or in a book such as this one.

Enjoy! – LInc.

iii

DOROTHY

Thirteen year old Dorothy was the youngest of widow Ella Knipstine's eight children. They were a poor family in the little town of Stinesville, but respected. For a girl in the seventh grade being poor made life somewhat difficult. That fall, with Thanksgiving at hand, things looked bleak in the Knipstine household.

As in past Thanksgivings, beans, cornbread and fried potatoes were certain to be the family's holiday fare, and she knew it. Dorothy also knew she and her siblings would be fortunate indeed to have that much, and she was truly thankful.

Yet, like all children at the approach of a day of feasting, she wished for more. As a prelude to the holiday she and her classmates at Stinesville School had been reading about the Pilgrims. Oh how they had feasted on the first Thanksgiving Day, and she yearned to emulate them, to share in a bounteous meal.

In a manner of speaking Dorothy had already shared in just such a meal. It happened while she sat at the table in the Knipstine kitchen one night doing her homework for English class. The assignment was a composition titled "Thanksgiving At Our House." In it pupils were required to describe what the coming festivities would be like at their individual homes.

Dorothy wrote about what she yearned most for on

Thanksgiving, a huge feast. She listed many tasty dishes to be served at her house along with the names of a collection of desserts which made her mouth water as she wrote them down.

At school the next day, when it was her turn to stand before the class and read her composition, Dorothy began, "I'm bored with turkey every Thanksgiving. This Thanksgiving we are going to have a big fat goose with dressing and gravy, and candied sweet potatoes and mashed potatoes, and corn and green beans."

There was a titter among her classmates, but Dorothy continued reading. She named the kinds of pies she'd always dreamed of having at Thanksgiving, and a yearned-for cobbler topped with ice cream. By this time the other children were laughing out loud. They knew the widow Knipstine was as poor as a church mouse and never did have a turkey for Thanksgiving, and she certainly could not afford to buy a big fat goose. They knew that Dorothy's composition was a fabrication. So did her teacher. Before the girl could finish reading her entire paper the teacher ordered her to sit down.

"Dorothy," the teacher admonished, "how can you lie like that? You know Jesus doesn't like liars. When you go home this afternoon you'd better kneel down and pray to Jesus to forgive you for telling such a lie."

Dorothy was crushed. She hadn't meant to lie to anyone. She had simply revealed the fondest Thanksgiving wish of a poor girl. She liked to write poems and stories so she had compiled a bit of fantasy, she had spoken aloud a dream. That Jesus might have been angry with her was more than she could bear, and she ran from the classroom, the school. Down the hill from the school building she ran, across town and to the railroad tracks.

She ran along the tracks to a small bridge that

spanned Jack's Defeat Creek at the edge of Stinesville. Constructed of creosoted heavy timbers and railroad ties, the bridge, remote and unpopular, provided the distraught girl a place of privacy and solitude. She sat and let her feet hang above the water below. She placed her arms on the lower bridge rail and rested her chin on the backs of her hands. And there in the context of her unintentional sin, the falsehood she had written and read to her class, she began contemplating Jesus.

Why would Jesus not like me, she wondered. She hadn't really told a lie. She had spoken only of things she hoped for, things she wished for. No one was hurt by what she had said. In her way she had only expressed a desire that life might be different for her, for her family. More than anything else her composition had been a prayer. How could it have been misinterpreted by Jesus? From infancy she had been taught that he was sweet and kind and loving, and that he understood little children. Why would he be angry?

Looking straight down over the lower rail into the water, Dorothy studied her reflection there. She wished the teacher had not charged her with a lie, had not humiliated her in front of all the other girls and boys. To herself she spoke a desperate wish her teacher might be wrong about Jesus. Although convinced of her innocence, she at last did as the teacher had recommended; she began praying to Jesus to forgive her.

In mid-prayer a sound attracted her attention and Dorothy raised her head. She was incredulous. Swimming down the creek toward her were three big wild geese. She thought she was dreaming. But after a second look she knew the geese were real. Then it struck the girl like a lightning flash, her wish for a big Thanksgiving dinner was being answered before her eyes.

Dorothy jumped to her feet and ran to the home of William Summitt, a youth who lived with his parents across the street from the widow Knipstine's home. After listening to her, William took down his rifle gun, accompanied her back to the bridge and shot the three geese.

The widow Knipstine took two of the geese and Dorothy and her siblings, as she had predicted before her class at school, did have goose meat and trimmings for Thanksgiving dinner. William took the third goose home for his mother to fix for their Thanksgiving dinner.

In later life Dorothy remembered this incident from her childhood as "The Geese From Heaven." A born story teller, she loved to recount her past in detailed oral narratives to her own children. Her husband, William Summitt, the same William Summitt who had shot the geese, was also one of her rapt listeners. This was only one of the stories she had told them.

On a sunny June day many years later, and only weeks after Dorothy had left this life, one of her children, Steve Summitt, related this story from memory as we strolled along the railroad tracks to the bridge where Dorothy had prayed to Jesus. Steve pointed out the place where his mother had sat dangling her feet over the creek below, and the bend in the creek where the three big wild geese had appeared. I was aware of an eerie yet calming sensation as he spoke, and for the briefest of moments I fully expected three big fat geese to swim into view.

"Mama's family was very poor," Steve said of his mother's early life, interrupting my thoughts. "When her father died and Grandmother Knipstine was faced with final expenses, she sat her children down and explained the seriousness of their situation. She told them they could keep the family milk cow but would have to the sell the house, or they could keep the house but have to sell the cow. They decided it was best to sell the family milk cow."

Dorothy was still a young girl when someone warned her mother, "Ellie, I think that Summitt boy has eyes for Dorothy."

It was true. William and Dorothy were falling in love. Whether the widow Knipstine believed it or not, she made no comment to her daughter. But when Dorothy and William went off to the county fair one summer day they learned that the path to bliss in their time was not an easy one. While riding hand in hand on the Ferris wheel they looked down to see a shocking sight. The widow Knipstine and William's father were ordering the attendant to stop the wheel.

"They made them get off," Steve remembered the account of that incident as it was told to him by his mother. "They had gone to the fair without permission, and Mama wasn't allowed to date yet. Mama said she got one of the worst switchings over that."

Only minutes before they climbed into a seat on the Ferris wheel Dorothy and William had visited a carnival photo booth and had their picture made together. It is one of two photos that accompany this story through the courtesy of their son Steve.

William was not discouraged. When after a basketball game one night he saw Uncle Winston kiss Dorothy, William put her on notice. "The next time you kiss anyone," he promised, "it'll be me." At sixteen Dorothy left school and went to work at RCA in Bloomington. She would spend twenty-six years there. In the meantime William kept his promise, he and Dorothy were married October 7, 1944. At the time of her passing, May 29, 1994, they had been married almost fifty years, their anniversary coming in October. She was survived by William and their four children.

Although she had quit school when she was still a

5

DOROTHY
At Sixteen

DOROTHY AND WILLIAM
At The Fair

mere girl, Dorothy, as a woman, was not quite finished with school. A loving mother and supportive of her children, she was a long-time member of PTO and had also served as president. While she never said that her childhood Thanksgiving recitation experience before her class had also influenced her interest in Richland-Bean Blossom schools, she readily accepted the challenge and was successful when she was urged to run in 1976 for a seat on the school board.

The first woman ever to be elected to that board, she was named secretary in 1977, and in 1978 was elected to a one-year term as president. She was re-elected to that post in 1979, and was re-elected to the school board in 1980 and 1984. The only school board member in the district's thirty-one year history to serve three terms, she also served three years as board president, three years as vice president, and five years as secretary.

Dorothy's death came at age sixty-seven after a lengthy illness. Her funeral service was conducted at Old Dutch Church on May 29. Bidding her farewell with her husband William, and her children, Larry, Mary Ellen Smith, Judy Arthur and Steve, and Dorothy's sister, Martha Bailey, were scores of mourners who filled the church to overflowing.

On that day in June, while her son Steve and I stood at the bridge over Jack's Defeat Creek where Dorothy as a child had prayed to Jesus, he remembered his mother's funeral service.

"May 29th was a beautiful day," he said. "The church doors and windows were open and the sunshine poured in. When they carried Mama to her grave the church bell was tolled sixty-seven times."

In a story which appeared in the *Ellettsville Journal* after her passing, Dorothy was extolled by Publisher Maurice E. Endwright as "A hard-working and dedicated board member, she always knew what was going

7

on. She fought hard to keep the Stinesville School open, (and) she worked for what was best for all students."

During her last term in office Dorothy was a leader in obtaining a controversial seven million dollar expansion of Edgewood High School, which included a year-round community swimming pool and an auditorium of more than a thousand seats. The effort, although successful, cost her a bid for a fourth term.

Despite her defeat the people of Richland-Bean Blossom acknowledged her years of service by naming a new giant, multi-purpose addition to the Stinesville Elementary School the "Dorothy Summitt Activity Center."

The addition, in the planning stage before her death, was completed almost a year later in March of 1995, the inscription appropriately chiseled for posterity into a limestone wall insert. It was a fitting tribute not only to a grand lady, but also to a young girl who might have had reason to remain bitter toward school but chose instead to serve and enhance the concept of public education.

The depth of Dorothy's fondness for Stinesville School was further revealed after her defeat for a fourth term in words she expressed to a school board member.

"Take care of my little school up there," she said.

THE STOREKEEPER

We met on the south side of the square – or is it the circle. Courthouse Square? Courthouse Circle? It could be either in Paoli. In reality it is more of a circle than it is a square. Anyone who has been in the courthouse, anyone who has shopped the stores around it, or just driven through the heart of town, would be inclined to agree: circle. Square?

That's where we met, on the south side of whatever it is. I introduced myself and, seemingly unimpressed, he informed me that he was on his way to lunch, and that our business, if we had any, would have to wait until after he ate.

"I'm on my way to the senior citizens," he spoke with cool directness. "They serve lunch over there every day for a dollar, and it's good. You can come with me and eat there, if you want – if you're sixty or over – or I'll see you when I'm finished."

I declined the dollar lunch and told him I'd see him when he was finished. More than fifty miles earlier someone had suggested I seek out Lloyd Hill. A traveling man who one day happened into the Hill Hardware Store in Paoli so enjoyed a friendly exchange with its owner that "Lloyd Hill," he later said to me, "is just what you're looking for."

Having never heard of the store, I unknowingly parked on the south side of the circle – square. Hill's

9

then was situated on the north side. Unless one drove it, there was only one other way from the south side to the north side – walk it – up an incline. And by the time I lugged myself and my camera gadget bag up that hill I was ready to sit, even lie down. But Hill's was closed.

It was later, after I had returned to the lower side of the square that someone of whom I had earlier inquired called out to me, "There's Lloyd now," and pointed to a tall, spare gentleman who was wearing a soft-brim brown hat, a brown cardigan over a flannel shirt and light cords.

"Excuse me," I spoke to him in greeting. And he proceeded to tell me what you've read above, that he was going to lunch and that I was welcome to join him. I should have. Thinking to grab a quick bite later I dashed off to kill another bird, so to speak. That project took so long that when I had finished with it I thought I should get back to Hill's. Foregoing my own lunch, then, I dumped my camera gadget bag into my car as I passed it on the south side of the square and climbed back up to the hardware store. Although I arrived in better physical condition this time I was again disappointed. The store was still closed.

I turned and looked back down the incline, then, and I saw a shocking sight. Mr. Hill was walking up the hill at a jaunty pace, stepping along as though the incline up which I had labored twice that noon wasn't there. And him eighty-four years old.

My shame knew no bounds. I bemoaned my poor physical condition, my throbbing heart, my weak lungs and my shaky legs that had let me down on that climb, while at the same time I stood in awe of what I beheld. But that's not all. When he got to where I stood waiting Mr. Hill announced without

10

the slightest hint of discomfort or dyspepsia that he'd had "beef stew, buttered cabbage, cottage cheese, a half pear, and iced tea," for lunch and that he was even then "full to my gizzard."

That was not all, either. While I tried to assimilate what I'd seen and heard, Mr. Hill unlocked the door to the store, went inside, filled up an ancient pipe from a pound tobacco tin, sat down in a padded metal chair, lit up, and began puffing clouds of stifling gray smoke out of his mouth.

"I had a good cook for forty-nine years," he said, his mind still on the pleasures of the past hour. "Till April eleventh, eleven years ago. I've never seen an old woman to take her place yet."

Her name was Pearl Pickens Hill. She had worked with him in a bakery they owned before they acquired the hardware store. A newspaper reporter had written a lengthy story about those earlier days. It appeared in a local paper with a photo of them. Mr. Hill had framed it and hung it on a wall in the store. Standing out from everything else in the story was the fact that Mr. Hill and his wife had reared two sons: Richard, who lived in Louisville, and Larry, whose home was down in Florida.

We visited for some time and while he spoke the fire in Mr. Hill's old pipe went out and he struck a long, wooden kitchen match to rekindle it.

"Started smoking when I was sixteen," he said puffing more gray clouds into the atmosphere. "If I hadn't of smoked I might of lived to be an old man."

He told me he'd been in business sixty years, thirty-five of which had been spent in the hardware store. It had been a lucrative stand, he said, until the one-stop shop stores arrived.

"Not anymore," he puffed on his pipe some more. "I don't do any business anymore. Competition is too

11

keen. This is just a place to loaf," he had taken the pipe out of his mouth and holding the bowl in the web of a thumb and forefinger he pointed the bit pistol-like around the store. "I use it for medicine. After coming down here all these years, if I didn't do it I'd go to seed. Folks'll say, 'Why don't you sell and get the money?' Well, what would I do with money? I've got a home. I wouldn't want to live with relatives and ruin their lives. I don't want to live in a condomini-um like some do. And I'd get tired of fishing after a while," he said.

From his seat in the padded lawn chair Mr. Hill had a clear view of the inclined sidewalk he had climbed so easily for an eighty-four year old man filled to his gizzard with stew. It was a pleasant pas-time to watch other people make the ascent. And every day he was in the store old friends would stop by to visit; one of them usually occupying the top step of a two-step ladder, on which I had sat during my visit, and the others standing around. And they talked.

The store was stocked with everything from a hog ring to "you name it," as Mr. Hill said. There were fishing tackle and lures enough to supply a legion of fishermen, and household needs enough to supply an army of homemakers.

"Two years ago you could've walked in here carry-ing a bicycle frame and in two hours you'd've been out in the street with a complete bicycle," he said. "But competition has ended all that too."

Mr. Hill had yielded to competition and no longer tried to compete. When he advertised it was, as he said, "Only what I do in the window," to attract passersby.

His philosophy might have been wrong, but that is the way he saw it, the way he wanted it then. Times were different from those days when Pearl was at his side and they baked and sold two loaves of bread for fifteen cents and cookies at twelve cents a dozen.

"All I need now is enough to pay my taxes, keep the business and the house up, buy my food and tend to my roses," Mr. Hill said.

LIZZIE PARSLEY

Of an advanced age, petite and bent, her smile frail and delicate, her azure eyes intense and alert, Lizzie Parsley was even in silence an eloquent testimony to her time and experience in Owensburg.

Our first meeting took place in Lehman's General Store. She walked in slowly, surveying a gathering of talkers and listeners as she approached. Standing at the edge of the group, weighing all that was said, she stood quietly, her eyes moving curiously from speakers to me, where I was seated taking notes. Satisfied, after a time, that I was being entertained by some of the town's story-tellers, she spoke.

"I'll tell you a story," she offered. Then shaking a threatening gnarled finger under my nose she warned, "But you must never put it in your paper that I told you, understand?"

To put a story in my paper was the reason I was in the general store. But out of curiosity I deferred to Lizzie and promised that so long as she lived and breathed I would not put the story she was about to tell in my paper.

"What I'm going to tell you happened a long, long time ago," she began. "But there might still be some-one around, someone besides me, who remembers. And I wouldn't want to hurt anybody's feelings. That's why I don't want you to put it in your paper. Agreed?"

I most certainly did agree, but some years later, when Lizzie attained the age of ninety, I visited with her at her home and obtained her permission to tell the story as she had related it to me and the loungers in the general store that day. This is how I remembered it.

"I was never so ashamed of myself," is what she said. "So ashamed. You know, sometimes you think you know all there is to know about a person, but in the end you can be all wrong. I know because I was. Oh, I was so wrong. And I am still ashamed.

"My husband was alive then and complaining of the stomach ache," the memory forced her lips back until they were in a straight line. "He was just sick all the time. We took him to the doctor and the doctor told him to drink a glass of dandelion wine every day until the condition cleared up.

"I didn't know anything about wine," she said. "Still don't, as far as that's concerned. I never took a drink in my life, or smoked, either. So I asked around and found a recipe for dandelion wine. We made some and put it in the root cellar, where it would stay cool. Besides, I didn't want any wine in the house.

"I don't remember when it was," she frowned as she tried to recall a point in time past, "but I began noticing that the wine was disappearing faster than I was taking it out of the bottle for my sick husband. I was just taking a little bit of it out of the bottle every day.

"Well," she shook her head, "at that time we were sharing our root cellar with a neighbor. So when I got to studying about it, I figured where the wine was going. I knew that he was nipping at it.

"Oh that upset me," she remembered her reaction. "That upset me so bad. When I'd see him, it didn't matter where, all I could think of was him stealing that dandelion wine. 'Thief!' I used to say to myself when I saw him. In the yard, at the store, in church, I'd see him and I'd think, 'Thief!' Have you ever had anybody steal from you?" she was suddenly erect, eyes snapping, demanding. "If you have then you know how I felt. And him a neighbor, right next door. A friend."

Lizzie paused to take a deep breath. "Well, I never said anything. How do you go to your next door neighbor and friend and say, 'You're stealing my husband's dandelion wine a drink at the time; wine that is medicine for him.' I just couldn't do that. I suppose I should have, for it got to be a big thing inside of me, and it was galling me.

"Then one day this man, he got sick and died," she said. "I didn't know what was wrong with him. Another doctor had taken my husband off of dandelion wine long before that, and I'd stopped making it, so I knew it wasn't the wine he'd been stealing that killed him.

"But," she shook her head, "I'll never forget looking down at him in his casket at the funeral home and thinking, 'Thief!' It was awful, but that's all I could think; and him alayin' dead like that. I tried to feel sorry for him but I couldn't. All that would come to mind was that he was a thief."

Lizzie was silent in thought for a few seconds. Then she calmly resumed her story.

"I don't quite remember," she said, "but it was several years later, when the whole family was visiting one day and we were sitting around the kitchen table having such a good time talking and laughing and I heard my son say, 'Some of the best fun we had was drinking Paw's bellyache medicine in the root cellar.'

"Well," said Lizzie, her blue eyes now clouded with pain at the ancient memory. "I couldn't believe my ears. I felt like the whole world had fallen in on me.

My own son and his friend had been drinking the dandelion wine all the time I was thinking our neighbor was stealing it."

In silence she slowly moved her gray head from side to side, perhaps in an attempt to shake away the painful memory.

Then she said,"I tried to ask the Lord to forgive me for how terribly wrong I'd been all those years, and for not having gone to our neighbor and friend in the first place and asked him about the missing wine. It's been years," she mused, her old head again moving from side to side, "but I'm still so ashamed of myself, and I wonder if I'll ever be forgiven."

I wondered about Lizzie's daily walks from her house to the post office and if it wasn't too much for a lady in advanced years. Lizzie said she'd walked all her life and that she used to walk three miles to attend church.

"We walked from the time we were kids, from the Martin County line clean into town," she said. "In the summer we'd walk barefoot till we got to a spring branch near the railroad tracks. We'd sit there and wash our feet in the cool water, then we'd put on our socks and shoes and go on to church."

Lizzie grew up in Martin County. After she married Edgar Parsley, they began housekeeping on Graded Road there, not too far from Greene County and Owensburg.

"After about three months we bought a house here in Owensburg for two hundred dollars, and I've been here ever since," she said.

Verdie Osborne owned the two-room structure, and he was pleased to accept a downpayment of twenty-five dollars from the newlyweds.

"Every three months we paid him another twenty-five dollars," Lizzie related the terms of the verbal contract. "We got it paid in two years. We paid it off by selling a cow and a hog. My Poppa,"she explained, "had given us a cow for our wedding present, along with an old hen and twenty-five chicks. And Poke Harp's dad, Sylvester, had given us a hog."

Lizzie and Edgar lived in the two-room house for many years afterwards. "We had four children," she said, "and they were all born in the same room – in the same bed in the same corner."

Sylvester Harp's gift of a hog was made of kinship; Edgar was reared by Uncle Nathan and Aunt Martha Harp. That made Lizzie a relative not only to Uncle Nathan and Aunt Martha, but also to John Harp, and his daughter, Ula, at Doan, and to Dennis (Snoog) Harp and Ora (Poke) Harp, and all the Harps around Owensburg.

"Aunt Marthy," Lizzie said, "was one of the best women that ever lived. And it was the greatest thing that ever happened in my life when I was able to care for her when she got down sick. In my house, I cared for her. She wouldn't come at first. She said, 'I'll not go. I'd like to, but I won't, unless Lizzie wants me, and asks me to come.' Well, I wanted her, and and I asked her, and I was so proud to ," Lizzie said.

"There was more love then," she reflected on people in her past. "Life was rougher, but there was more love then than there is now. We worshiped God then, too. And we helped the sick. We cared for one another. And there wasn't the meanness in the world that there is now."

She suddenly remembered something else.

"My Poppa would get down with the *pneumony*, and the menfolks around would come in and cut Poppa's wood. People gave time and work to help then, and the work was a lot harder than now," she said.

Lizzie reared her family cooking on a wood range

that was so low in construction it had to be adjusted in height for her use by placing three bricks under each leg.

"We bought that thing off an old man for five-dollars, and he threw in a bread pan and an old iron tea kettle for boot," she recalled. "I cooked on that for a good bit," she said, noting that it was almost all her life, "before I got a coal oil stove. But,"she hurried to add, "I still hung on to the old wood stove. Food cooked on it had a different flavor – it was better."

Edgar died shortly before he and Lizzie would have celebrated sixty years together. A disabled veteran of World War I, Edgar was buried in the town cemetery, not too distant from where Lizzie lived and where she went to church. She and Edgar never owned – or drove – an automobile, and they walked every place they ever went, unless someone gave them a ride in a wagon. It was not surprising that after a lifetime of walking Lizzie should have begun tiring.

"Seems like it's just twice as far from me as it used to be," she said of postmaster Wilma Rollins' brick working place. "I have to cross the town branch, climb up the hill, walk all the way across town, cross another branch – why," she exclaimed with a sigh, "it's right at a quarter of a mile."

After a pause, Lizzie sighed, "When the weather is pretty – sometimes – I can enjoy it."

Whatever the distance, whatever the weather, Lizzie would not be denied her mail. When she was unable to get to the post office she relied on the same diamond in the rough who had cut kindling and packed coal for her every day the previous winter, her son-in-law, Earnest Page, to help her.

"No one," Lizzie testified, "could ask for anyone to be better than he is."

Putting it all together, life in Owensburg – includ-

Lizzie Parsley

ing regular visits to the town cemetery – was still attractive to Lizzie.

"It's pretty sad, going over there," she said of the cemetery. "It's a sad place. There are so many people over there who I know. But it's nice that they are not very far from me. And my church is right close by – the Missionary Baptist. And the general store, and, of course, the post office. It's pretty marvelous," she insisted, "that you can do all those things and never own a car – never have to drive."

On the day she released me from my promise, Lizzie had received several greeting cards in her box at the post office, bringing the total for the week of her ninetieth birthday to one hundred and fifty-eight.

"Lawsey!" she exclaimed as she recounted her bewilderment at the deluge of good wishes. "I never did get more that four or five birthday cards on my birthday. I was surprised."

The cards were not her only surprise. On the night of her birthday David Atkins, her Sunday school teacher, picked her up to take her to his house for supper. It was a cagey move for a Sunday school teacher. Instead of taking Lizzie home Atkins took her to the church where her Sunday school class secretly awaited with numerous gifts and a large cake on which stood a single large candle. It was such a pleasant surprise that Lizzie, who had cherished the hope of living until she reached ninety, revealed a new wish.

"Now I'd like to live till I'm a hundred," she told the gathered well-wishers. It was a wish none would deny her, capped with the traditional Happy Birthday song.

"I never gave anything like that a thought," Lizzie said of the surprise. "Boy! I never was so shocked in my life. We had a big supper. We visited, there were some cameras there, I had my picture taken with Merlie Craig, our minister, and we had a good time."

Lizzie certainly was not a movie or television star or a famous person that she should have received all those birthday cards and gifts. She was just a kind, simple lady who was born at Sand Hill in Martin County and who had lived in tiny Owensburg most of her life. She had shared in the happiness of living there, the town's many births, graduations and weddings. And in her years as a good neighbor and friend she had trekked countless times from her home to the general store to deposit in the used cigar box on the counter her contribution to buy floral wreaths for those who had preceded her to glory.

She had taught Sunday school for many years and for years she led the singing at church services. On the occasion of her ninetieth birthday she was the town's oldest resident. Despite that she still walked to get her mail almost every day. She attended Sunday school when she was able, and she walked to the store. If the weather was suitable she took the weekly bus to the Senior Center in Bloomfield to spend a day with friends.

"It's not bad," Lizzie said of her birthday and having reached the age of ninety. "I am a little slower, and my mind doesn't work as good as it used to, but other than that it's no different."

THE PIGGERY

If you've never choked over a cleaning sponge soaked in ammonia you may not be able to imagine the violent sensation of walking from a clear brisk March morning into a farrowing barn of eighty-two brood sows and seven hundred little pigs.

Like the full-bodied pungency of ammonia, the malodorous air you breathe in a farrowing barn stays with you for hours. If you're unlucky, as I was unlucky, the length of time the stink stays around is also determined by whatever you may pick up on the soles and heels of your shoes.

The heady experience is worth whatever misery may come of it, though. For example, a tour of a piggery is educational; impressively so. While you're gasping for a breath of fresh air, and coaxing your breakfast to stay where you put it a couple hours earlier, you learn many interesting facts about where the chops and bacon you eat come from. And you promise yourself you'll never eat chops and bacon again, ever.

Included in the facts are the stages of pig life. Pigs are not always pigs, you should know. No sir. After eight weeks a girl pig, so long as she remains a miss, is a gilt. And a boy pig becomes a shoat. Not all girl pigs remain gilts. Those that do, as soon as they are old enough, go to market. Those few gilts that are lucky enough to stay home become mother pigs, or sows.

The way I understood it, few boy pigs are fortunate

enough to grow from being shoats into being boars. Usually early in life a surgical blade transforms a boy pig into a barrow. Such a procedure renders him to a status of something akin to a wheelbarrow with the wheel hopelessly broken off it. The surgical process also has a drastic mental effect on him; it adjusts his thinking from amorous companionship with girl pigs to rooting in the ground for grubs, and grunting and snorting until such time as he too goes to market.

The real pleasures that come from being born a boy pig, you soon learn during a visit to a piggery, are reserved for those pigs that are allowed to grow into boars. Enviably, all they do is eat, sleep, and breed, eat, sleep, and breed; a euphoric cycle that goes on and on until they are unable to breed any longer. And off they go to market, sad to have the good times end so soon.

Meandering around a farrowing barn also makes it easier to understand why some people will adopt a little pig as a pet. They appeared to be the cutest little animals as they trotted up and down the long rows of farrowing crates in which their mothers lay. Charging over the pine shavings-covered floor they darted into one farrowing crate after another. There they visited the mothers of their little friends, or visited their little friends who were dining or asleep stacked like ricked wood under huge heating lamps. It is then you realize that if one little pig is cute, seven hundred of them will send you into adoptive ecstasies.

You wonder, too, with seven hundred little pigs darting about, how a mother sow can tell which little pigs are hers. But they know, and a little thief who dares to latch onto the mother of a friend is sent away squealing in fright. If, because of the overall stink of a piggery, you think all pigs smell alike, I was informed by the manager of the hog farm that a brood sow can ascertain her own pigs by their individual pig odor.

The manager's name was Isaac Foster. He said he'd

been raising pigs for fifteen years. Before that he did a stint in the Army, worked in a factory, drove a bread truck, and did other kinds of work. He said of raising pigs, "I like this better."

It was not easy work. While the eighty-two sows in the farrowing barn nursed their seven hundred little pigs, that many more sows were pregnant and would occupy the farrowing crates when the seven hundred little pigs reach six weeks. The little pigs would then be moved into a nursery in another barn. Meanwhile another eighty-two sows were nearing breeding time, and the cycle revolved perpetually, keeping Foster and thirteen boars almost constantly on their toes.

"When piggin' time comes," Foster said of one of his subsidiary roles as manager, "this is a day and night job. You stay with the sows when the pigs start to come. And if a sow can't have her pigs you've just got to go get them. A sow is just like anything else. There's nothing ever has young but what it doesn't have trouble sometime. You pull a pig just like anything else. I don't know if a doctor pulls a baby like that, but I suppose he would."

I asked Foster if his wife ever scolded him for forgetting to take off his boots before going into the house. He said her name was Eva, and he said a nice thing about her.

"Yeah," he first answered my question with a smile. Then he added, "She has to have a lot of understanding I reckon." And then he said, "If I'm in trouble at piggin' time she gets right out here and helps me. She's all right."

The Fosters had four children and the eldest, a son, enjoyed working alongside his father. "The two youngest ones," Foster shook his head, "are generally up on that hill over yonder riding their ponies when I want them."

"Do you have to get used to this odor? Do you ever get used to it?" I asked.

"Never," Foster replied. "You never actually get accustomed to it. After you're in here a while it ain't so bad. But if you go out and come back, you have to get used to it all over again."

"Must be awful," I groaned.

"No, not really," Foster smiled. "It's not so bad. Today it smells like money. The price of hogs today is twenty-eight cents."

PUNKIN CENTER

Someone once said that if Ad Gray were ordered to bed he'd have to be hog-tied to keep him there.

"That's right," the old sage of Punkin Center said for himself. "I wouldn't stay down."

Not for more than five days, anyway. That's how long he once allowed himself to be downed at the Bedford Medical Center.

"I got a little dizzy. My heart, I guess," he said of the reason he was there.

That was the news that had reached my desk at the newspaper and taken me to that popular place on Tater Road in Orange County: "Ad Gray's had a heart attack."

In a swinging chair in the middle of what he and his beloved Mabel call their "museum," Ad at eighty-three, appeared none the worse for the experience.

"Too much mouse-trap cheese," Mabel admonished.

"I love it," Ad admitted.

Delivered from Wisconsin in large Daisy rounds the cheese was one of a handful of items sold in the Grays' store.

"Long before I ever started up here, three old stores carried it," Ad said. "One at Millersburg, and one at Chambersburg, and at Catlin Brothers at Leipsic. Must have been 1912-1915. Farmers came to pick up fertilizer and they'd buy it for lunch, five-cents worth

Ad and Mabel Gray

with crackers. If the kids happened to be along they bought ten cents worth. It sold for twenty cents a pound. Now it's two dollars and forty-five cents."

Ad's voice rose in pitch as he dragged out the words of the current price of the popular cheese he'd been selling at Punkin Center for more than sixty-three years.

"Came here in January 1922," he would inform visitors, using as few words as possible. "This was a two-room log house."

At some point he became a collector. The store, the adjoining garage, the surrounding yard, every place one might have looked was occupied with the strange and rusted fruits of that endeavor.

"That's why I won't stay down," Ad said. "You can't be closed up with all this junk here, if you want people to see it."

From around the U.S., they came to see it. From Europe and South America, too, according to Ad's register. And all any of them could buy was a cut of mouse-trap cheese, maybe a bar of candy, and a six-ounce Coke in a glass bottle to wash it down.

"It's my trademark," Ad said of the cheese. "I've been selling it here ever since January 25, 1922."

More than a decade after that beginning, Ad met twenty-one year old Mabel at a farm sale.

"Sometime later I said something to her and she said, 'I don't know', and then she said something to me and I said, 'I don't know,' then we went to sparking," Ad said of the beginning of their courtship.

"I don't know what happened after that," Mabel observed, "But one Saturday we went to old John McCullough's, the preacher. It was arainin', and the thunder and lightnin' was abangin' outside, and with a scared old dog standing between us, the preacher married us. Next morning we set out for Chicago and the World's Fair."

29

"See," Ad smiled, "I haven't kept Mabel working all the time."

Among the couple's collectibles was a four-cylinder 1922 Gray Roadster.

"Fellow one day said if it was in mint condition he could get me fifty-thousand for it," Ad said. "But I told him if I sold it, then I wouldn't have a Gray car.

"We just won't sell anything but cheese, candy bars and Cokes," he repeated. "But someone always tries to buy something. We have all this stuff here for people to come and look at. We just ain't hardly that hard up enough to sell yet. This ain't a store anyway. It's a museum."

The store – or museum – was also "a place where old times are talked." Times such as the Thirties, when banks closed and Ad, along with tens of thousands of other Americans, was left without operating capital.

"My brother, Byron had a mare he sold for a hundred dollars to a man who carried his money in his overalls." Ad recalled how Punkin Center survived that closure. "And my brother turned to me and said, 'You can have this hundred dollars to see you through,' And it did."

Old Sime Locust, a fiddler of some repute, who worked his land and played his fiddle at a big doings at old man Cornell's was talked there too, to use Ad's idiom. And Bruce Gray, the patriarch of the Gray clan, who made his way to Orange County from Newport, Tennessee, was also talked there. And there was always the story about how the present building came to be.

"Hard to believe," Ad said. "But there's the contract hanging right up there," he pointed to a framed document hanging on a wall. "Kern Shrum put in the basement – twenty-four feet by forty feet – and laid up the blocks nine feet high for a total of forty-eight.

30

"That's not all," he continued. "Shrum brought an expert concrete man who worked all day for three dollars."

"Everything in here has a story," Mabel said. "Either where it came from, whose it was and how come us to have it."

Those stories were available to visitors every day from morning 'til night. Take the one about the Stampers Creek bridge, for example. It was probably the first time that anything quite like it had happened in Orange County. It most certainly was the last time that anything quite like it will happen in Punkin Center. One reason being there was no other ninety-two year old bridge over Stampers Creek at that point, another being there was no other Ad Gray in that tiny community or, for that matter, in the whole of Orange County.

For awhile it appeared that it might not even have happened the one time, which was in 1972. After Ad learned that the old bridge was to be replaced he offered county commissioners twenty-five dollars for it. They held out for seventy-five. To Ad it was just another trinket to display with the scores of collectibles at the famous Gray place. He was willing to wait.

When his offer was at last accepted Ad invited a host of friends to the moving ceremony. He and Mabel arranged a Dutch lunch of hot dogs, rat-trap cheese and soft drinks.

"Well," Ad remembered that day, "when it came right down to moving that bridge up here, I was able to do it by myself with the farm tractor with the manure spreader on it. And I didn't need any help. When I realized that I told them they could all go home. And they said, 'We aren't leaving until we've eaten all those hot dogs and rat-trap cheese and drunk up all the pop.' So I had to put up with them a little longer," he concluded the narration with a laugh that seemed to mean I could believe what he had said or not believe it.

Moved forty rods from where it had stood since 1880, the bridge became part of the quietly popular tourist attraction.

Then there was Ad's story of how long his museum had been attracting the curious.

"In 1809 a man came from North Carolina to Leesville and he killed a deer, skinned it and slept under the hide that winter," he said. "In the spring he returned to North Carolina, gathered his wife and family, some other families, and came back to Leesville and settled there.

"They planted crops and at harvest time they hauled potatoes through here on the way to market. And the trail, that road out there," Ad pointed, "was called Tater Road."

In later years, the story continued, Ad's parents settled there. Acres of pumpkins planted and harvested by his father led to the name Punkin Center. And still later, in 1922, Ad opened a cream station in a two room house there.

"Bromer," he said of other nearby communities, "was going good then, and Syria, too, and folks said, 'Ad can't do no good,' but there's nothing at Bromer and Syria now and here I am."

When the Grays marked the museum's sixtieth anniversary, large numbers of friends and past and new visitors arrived to celebrate with the food and drink for which the Gray's had become famous.

The name Ad had no known origin, Ad revealed, except that its bestowal upon him may have been influenced by the fact that Ad Tow and Ad McCoy once lived in that rural community.

"And," Ad added the inevitable, "they thought that I'd never be able to spell so they just called me Ad."

He did learn to spell. But after his graduation from high school in 1921 it appeared that his formal education had come to an end.

"I wanted to be a teacher, "Ad remembered. "But my dad was against school. A boy we knew had gone to college and my dad had heard that he'd been drunk, and that he had cussed and smoked cigarettes. So he told me, 'You're not going to college. You'll just be drinking and cussing and smoking there.' My dad was from Tennessee, and he came here in 1898 and believed in work on the farm, no school. I was lazy. I didn't want to farm. And he finally saw that and let me go to college," he said.

Only twelve weeks of study were required to obtain a teaching license. Ad got his, returned to Punkin Center, taught as a substitute for a few days and never again saw the inside of a classroom.

"I just loafered up at the store where Dad sold ice cream," he laughed. "Then I talked him into buying a two room house that used to set right there," he pointed to a small area within the museum.

"We used to buy everything on credit in those days," he said. "Buy one week, pay the next. And that first invoice I got from my wholesale supplier, Wheeler-Foutch, was for three hundred and twenty-four dollars. That's what we started with."

After more than forty-five years of operation, the store at Punkin Center was discontinued. The Grays did, however, continue selling rat-trap cheese and Cokes. The twenty-two inch in diameter rounds of cheddar were still popular with visitors (some one hundred the Sunday before my visit) and several rounds were sold each tourist season.

As always, there was much to see at Ad's and

Mabel's place; there was always a phase of their long experience awaiting listeners. Good listeners, Ad once gave directions to Punkin Center, should turn east at Orleans or Paoli to Tater Road. However, he cautioned them to not expect too much from Punkin Center.

"There's not too much happening here, only fun," he said.

It was not so popular a place that everyone knew of it. Those who dialed information and asked their telephone operator for Punkin Center, Indiana, might very well have heard her reply with a puzzled, "Where?"

How could they have possibly known that there was such a place, and that it was situated on scenic Tater Road south of Stamper's Creek at the point of a V lying on its side with its angles opening westward to Plattsburg at the top and Kossuth at the bottom?

Two houses, each with its own business enterprise attached, made up Punkin Center, the one owned by Ad and Mabel, and the other owned by Bert and Evelyn Gray, Ad's brother and sister-in-law. Like his brother, Bert had his share of stories to tell about Punkin Center. One that I thought should be preserved was his version of how the place got its name.

"Well," he began narrating it one day, "we had the whole bottomland in punkins," and he waved a hand in the direction of lush, green acres of lowlands. "And we had the awfullest pile of punkins from that. I never saw so many punkins in all my life. They brought us more than a thousand dollars. That was a lot of punkins at that time. Why, it took twenty wagon loads to fill one of those semi trucks. You wouldn't have believed it if you had seen it. That was the year my brother Ad took a notion to open a store across the road here. And it was Ad that named this place Punkin Center because of all those punkins that year." And for posterity he added, "Maybe they tell the story that we got all those punkins from one seed and one vine because it sounds good, I don't know. But we got those punkins from more than any one seed or any one vine, I'll tell you."

Bert split his time between farming and sharing with Evelyn the pleasures of antiquing. Together they collected all manner of antiques – cherry corner cupboards, cord beds, pie safes, Cranberry glassware, chests, washstands, just to name a few (a very few) – for fifteen years. They filled their house, then filled an outbuilding, then Bert built a building thirty by twenty feet and they filled that, and then the overflow made its way into the barn. Then they began selling some of it.

"We didn't aim to sell nothing," Bert said of their enterprise. "But the house and everything else got so full it was a case of moving out or selling. So we started selling."

During a Dogwood Festival at Orleans, Bert and Evelyn consented to opening their doors as one of three "Houses On Tour" in conjunction with the festivities.

"Between one o'clock in the afternoon until about six there were several hundred people come through here," Bert said. "You never saw the like of so many people."

They may never have consented to another such arrangement, but Bert and Evelyn were the kind of people who would drop everything just to show visitors their possessions. And, if the notion struck them, they might have sold some.

After leaving Punkin Center that day I found a note in my pocket which read, "Punkin Center: Pop. Five and one-third." I'd forgotten to have either Ad or Bert explain the "one-third," so I tried telephoning them.

35

That's when I got a puzzled "Where?" from information operators in exchanges at Bloomington, French Lick, Seymour, Salem and New Albany. I never did reach them.

FERTILIZER NIGHTMARE

An inquiry as to which fertilizer might induce spring flowers to grow and blossom more abundantly brought an unexpected answer from a Brown County man who seemed to be having repeated success with his flower and vegetable gardens.

"Chicken manure," Richard McNew replied without hesitation. "Spread it in your flower beds now. In the spring you'll have nice flowers. Lots of them. Put it around your tomato plants and you'll have big, red, juicy tomatoes."

Chicken manure? Where would we get it? There wasn't a chicken in our neighborhood that we knew of. We'd heard a rooster every so often, especially when I stood on the back stoop outside our kitchen door and whistled up our cats for dinner. From somewhere in the distance the rooster would give me his raucous reply. "Err-err-err-yeach!" He must have had a throat problem for it was a terrible sound. I'd whistle, the rooster would crow. The cats came, too. But chicken? Never. Where would anyone find that many chickens?

"Let me tell you," said Mr. McNew. And he recounted an incredible tale about a springtime trip he once made with a friend to a distant poultry farm. The object: to obtain a pickup truckload of chicken manure for his friend's vegetable garden.

"The stuff is free if you load it yourself," Mr. McNew

continued with his account. "If you have them load it the cost is only five dollars. They use a front-end loader. One scoopful and you'll have enough chicken manure to cover all the garden you'll ever have."

His friend apparently was not convinced of that. He insisted on two scoopfuls in his half-ton pickup truck. The overload pushed the truck bed down within a hair of the tops of the rear tires. The front wheels, meanwhile, reared up, barely touching the pavement.

At this point I interrupted Mr. McNew's narrative to tell him of a similar experience. My wife and I had taken our minitruck one afternoon to a rural sawmill to buy enough native lumber with which to build a deck on our house. We loaded the long boards by hand and it was dark before we could start our return trip.

As we drove from the sawmill property onto the blacktop highway I was aware that I could barely see the road. I checked the light switch. It was on. I pushed it off and then back on. The roadway was still barely visible.

"I hate to tell you this," I said worriedly to my wife. "But something's wrong with our headlights. We're forty miles from home, we are carrying a truckload of lumber, and we have no lights."

Panic gripped me. What to do? I worked the light switch again and again. Then I heard my wife.

"There they are," she called out. "Up there."

I looked up through the windshield. Sure enough the light beams were up there – illuminating electric and telephone wires and the tops of utility poles. And then I remembered. When I had turned from the sawmill property onto the highway the steering had seemed weird. Then it dawned on me. We had so over-loaded the small truck the front wheels were almost off the ground.

It was a scary trip, but we managed to get home

safely that night. In Mr. McNew's case it was different, as the continuation of his account of the chicken manure adventure revealed.

"Two front-end loader scoopfuls of chicken manure is a lot of chicken manure," he said informatively while making facial expressions to reinforce his point. "It was black, and wet, and feathers stuck out all over it, and oh!" Mr. McNew scrunched up his face while he shook his head from side to side, "It stank!" He shrugged as though to rid himself of the memory. "Anyway," he resumed his story, "six miles out the road and the right rear axle snapped in two, pitching us, truck and chicken manure into a ravine."

Luckily they were alive and unhurt. And just as luckily, a junkman acquaintance of Mr. McNew's happened to come along in one of those flat tilt-bed trucks on which cars are winched and hauled away. After examining the plight of the disabled chicken manure-loaded truck the junkman agreed to help. Together the three of them labored and sweat and eventually the pickup and its odious load were out of the ravine and on the junkman's truck, and they started off. Two miles further down the road they stopped and rewarded themselves with a case of cold beer.

"Six more miles farther down the road," Mr. McNew said, "and we suddenly felt the truck pitch and go faster. We turned around to look and we saw that the pickup had slipped off the tilt-bed. It was bouncing wildly around back there in the middle of the highway, chicken manure flying all over the place, and cars trying to dodge all that shi-stuff and the bouncing pickup."

The driverless manure-loaded missile at last came to a halt without killing, hurting or dirtying anyone. By this time the broken axle was compounded by a damaged transmission and driveshaft. They had been practically sheared in the pickup's slide backward off the junkman's tilt-bed truck.

Working as best they could around the splatterings of chicken manure, Mr. McNew and his friends re-winched the pickup truck onto the tilt-bed truck. When they finally arrived at the junkman's place of business the cold beer had been consumed to within eight warm cans of the whole case. They set about repairing the pickup anyway.

They found a usable rearend on a junked truck that was several years older than the one loaded with chicken manure. It was geared lower, too, but it would work; and they began installing it on the broken down pickup. It took the rest of the day and the warm beer to do it, but they did it. And it worked.

It was at this time that a friend of the junkman happened by and offered to purchase what was left of the overload of chicken manure. They made a deal with him for half and he loaded it by the shovelful himself into a four-wheel drive pickup and hauled it away.

"We spent the night at the junkyard and slept on an old couch that was dirty with grease and oil," Mr. McNew continued. "By that time we were pretty dirty ourselves and we fit right into the surroundings."

Next day still another friend drove them a hundred miles in search of a used transmission. They finally found an older model and returned to the junkyard. Then it was bedtime, and for a second night unwashed, unshaved, still wearing the same clothes, and still far from home, Mr. McNew and his friend again slept on the oil and grease stained couch in their junkyard haven.

"The next day we learned that the guy with the four-wheel drive pickup truck got stuck with his chicken manure in a soybean field," Mr. McNew said. "He had to get a semi-wrecker to pull him out. From the kind of luck everyone was having with that stuff, I don't know," he shook his head vigorously at the memory, "but I got to thinking that, unlucky as we'd all been with it, maybe instead of chicken manure we'd picked up a load of ghost manure."

On the third day of their adventure Mr. McNew and his friend installed the transmission on the broken-down half-ton pickup. The third night was also spent at the junkyard office. The fourth day found them waiting from early morning to late afternoon at an Indianapolis firm that custom made driveshafts.

Still unwashed and unshaved late on the fifth day they rode the pickup, with less than half the original load of chicken manure they had started with, into Bloomington.

"When I got home everybody wanted to know where I'd been for so long," Mr. McNew sighed at the recollection. "I was never so exhausted, so I just told them, 'It's a long story.' But as the years went by it got funnier. And my friend did have a nice garden that summer.

"But," Mr. McNew shook his head, "he could have bought a freezer and all the food he could eat in five years for what that load of chicken manure cost him."

SIMMERMAN'S STORE

If you've never seen large chunks of ice "growing" in trees, you should visit Williams on a cold winter's day after the White River East Fork has been rampaging sixteen feet over the dam there.

"That's what it looked like," avowed Mary Simmerman. "There were great big chunks of ice way up in the trees lining the river, just like they were growing in them."

We were in Simmerman's Store and Jake, Mary's husband, had brought out a record book and was pointing to an entry in it. "See here," he said, a finger tapping a page. "On February 5th the river was running sixteen and three-tenths feet over the dam. That's when it was."

Jake's river-level log began with the year 1913, the time of the big flood, when the East Fork of the White River rose thirty-one feet over the dam. In 1937, the year of another big flood, according to Jake's log, the water rose twenty-five feet. On May 12, 1961 it was twenty-two and four-tenths feet. March 10, 1963, water was sixteen and eight-tenths feet; March 14, 1964, nineteen and eight-tenths feet; and on March 29, 1968, eighteen and two-tenths feet over the dam. "Right now," Jake said of Wednesday, April 7, 1982, "I'd say the river is running about four feet over the dam."

With the river level at that height the roads leading

Williams Dam At Flood

in and out of Williams were clear of flood water and there was no immediate danger to me, not even of getting my feet wet. For that reason I felt brave enough, as did other curious visitors to the popular dam town that day, to take my chances with the rising river, and with "Max," Jake and Mary's *superdog.*

Simmerman's Store was housed on the first floor of the second most imposing structure in Williams, the dam being the most imposing. Situated on the incline of a hill, the brick building was rectangular in shape. On the lower level of the hill, two sides of the building rose sharply to three stories. On the upper level of the hill, the remaining two sides were two stories high. The store was on the ground level of the two-story sides, one side of which comprised the front of the building. Thousands of bricks made up the total structure, and native limestone quoins outlined its facade. In the small river town setting the building was an eye-catching, if incongruous, sight.

Simmerman's could be reached by walking or driving up to it, or by walking or driving down to it, depending on the direction from which a visitor approached. A wide concrete patio stretched across its front, and it was on the patio that Max, emitting threatening barks and ominous growls, trotted out as a bare-toothed welcoming committee of one to freeze me in fear. He sniffed me front and back, and satisfied that I was friendly, the animal eventually allowed me to pass, weak-kneed, into the store. "He'll bark like that to let us know that there is someone around, but he won't bite," Jake said, hoping to calm my fear.

Max at that time had shared with the Simmerman's nine of the thirty years they had the store. It was something of a relief to think they should know their dog well enough to believe he would not bite. At least not in the daytime, and not when there are other peo-

Simmerman's Store

ple around, as Jake also went on to say. It might have been nicer had Max had a sign hanging from his neck announcing that message.

"He's an awful good watchdog," Jake continued with a disarming smile. "He always lets us know when there's someone around. He's a good dog."

That was not a guarantee that good dog Max wouldn't take a leg off a nocturnal visitor, Jake went on to warn. Max did not take kindly to nighttime callers, he said. Since I wasn't planning to be in Williams after dark, I decided that I might be safe. "He looks like a *superdog* to me," I told Jake while I studied the canine face that seemed to be smiling at me from a package of Superdog Something or Other on a display shelf. "What breed is he, anyway?"

Jake arched his brows and raised his shoulders as if to say that Max's pedigree was questionable. Calling on my limited knowledge of dog breeds, I formed an opinion. At the risk of Max reading my mind and possibly eating me up in anger, I deduced that, from his appearance, Superdog was not a candidate for registration in the AKC. A little on the shaggy side, he appeared to have strong German Shepherd influences, although he was considerably shorter than a German Shepherd. His lack of height stemmed from obviously stunted legs, which were strangely shorter in the back than in the front. For a dog, he had a funny way of sitting on the patio. The tall store windows and double doors were inset between four reaching limestone columns. The limestone slab that formed the step leading into the store continued on each side of the doorway to effect an architectural bench some seven or eight inches in height under each window. It was in the far corner of that bench, to the left of the doorway, that Max parked his carcass after he had finished with me. He reclined with his haunches on the bench and his forepaws planted on the patio floor below. So much had it been his favorite place to recline, he had worn a slight depression in the limestone slab. He no doubt had his reasons for standing in the front and lying in the back like that. Because of his shorter back legs, he may have been more comfortable in that position.

Perhaps he had been too often exposed to humans who hunkered on those slabs and he was trying to emulate them. One thing was for certain, in that position, Max was a comical sight. But in deference to his earlier greeting, I did not laugh.

The Simmermans had two sons, Gordon and Kenneth, who grew up in the store. Jake and Mary were younger then, and Williams was a busy place. Classes were still being conducted in the town's school. Residents and neighboring farmers bought their groceries at the store. Monroe Reservoir was still in the future and fishermen in large numbers came from four states to fish above and below the dam. It was a lucrative time for the Simmermans. Jake remembered that business was so good he and Mary spent two-thirds of every day in the store serving customers.

"So much had to be done then that it now seems we had our children such a short time while they were children," Mary said dolefully. Jake shook his head in silent, thoughtful agreement.

BOBBY SHAW

One hallowed week when the nation's newspapers were tooting their horns, the name of Bobby Shaw stood out as an important contributor to the success of American newspapering. But Bobby's name stood out that week only in Bedford, Indiana, for it was in that Lawrence County town that his contribution was made. And it stood out only because I chose to write about him.

Bobby was handing out packages of political book matches to Bedford businessmen for mayoral aspirant Robert H. Adamson when I stopped for this interview. He carried the packages in a time-worn graying *Daily Times Mail* carrier bag slung around his neck.

The bag was so big it almost concealed the faded green galluses with rusted metal snaps that held up Bobby's baggy gray pants and pressed into the front of his faded plaid shirt. He squinted through thick, wire-framed lenses that were shaded along with his round face by the long bill of a sweat-stained gray cap.

"They won't let me carry papers anymore," Bobby said, shifting the bag to the front of his short body so that he could better sit down. "And I never missed delivering a paper to a customer, and I always put it right in between the doors."

49

Bobby may be remembered in Bedford as the man who carried the *Indianapolis Star, Louisville Courier-Journal, Indianapolis News,* the now defunct Bloomington *Courier-Tribune* and, once, the Bedford *Daily Times-Mail.*

"When I carried papers," he said in recollection of happier days, "at Christmas it was just terrible (meaning wonderful). Oh it was just miserable (meaning marvelous). I'd get so many tips. One year I got a hundred dollars."

"But," he said, squinting at me through his thick lenses, "I gave good service, and I never missed delivering a paper in my life."

Bobby at this time was forty-six. He was born in Orleans, in Orange County, where he attended five grades of elementary school. It was shortly after completing the fifth grade that he arrived in Bedford, where he lived with his mother until she died three years before I stopped him for this talk.

"I've got a nice room over at Kate Mosier's," he said of his new home at a rooming house at 1629 J Street, in Bedford. "It's right across the street from Robbins' Flats."

Robbins' Flats was the popular name for the county jail, then under the control of county sheriff Farrell Robbins. Kate Mosier's was across 17th St. from the jail. Depending on who was sheriff at the time, Bobby had his own pet name for the jail. For example, when Levi Hatfield was sheriff Bobby called the place Hatfield's Hotel.

Through struggling boyhood and well into struggling manhood, Bobby carried and delivered newspapers. I was unable to learn from him why the papers discontinued his services. Anyway, he had never been honored for his contribution to the newspaper business during a National Newspaper Week, not until I wrote this column about him.

Bobby had been more than just a newspaper carrier. Somewhere within his unexplainable self, Bobby coveted a profound love for newspapering, an excitement for the major story, in news and in sports. Had he not been deprived of an education I felt he might have become a reporter or a sportswriter. His room at Kate's was a virtual newspaper morgue, stacked with scrapbooks filled with the pastings of years of patiently selected newspaper clippings.

"If ever you need to know anything about a major story," he offered this mammoth contribution to newspapering through me to the newspapers of the nation, "come to my room at Kate's. I've got it."

Few people knew about that. Fewer cared. But Bobby was more than just a newspaper carrier. If you saw him walking down the street you couldn't even begin to guess what he might be carrying in the big bag.

"I've carried just about everything in this old bag," he said, giving the aged bag a heist. "I pass out handbills, all kinds of advertising things, and advertising for politicians, and I carry all that stuff in here."

"He's a hustler," a professional man said of Bobby's spirit, and his application to his work. "You can count on him to deliver every single handbill."

"He's probably one of the best liked people in town," another said.

The feeling seemed to be mutual.

"Just name one person in Bedford, and he'll be good," Bobby said in his limited vocabulary of the people of the town. "They're all good. They're fine people here." Then he squinted through his thick lenses again, and he added with a touch of disappointment, "Of course some of them backed the St. Louis Cardinals, though."

Baseball, and the boxing ability of "Cassius Clay" — whom Bobby refused to recognize as Muhammad Ali

— were his passions. And he took a great deal of pleasure from listening to country music with Bill Mack in Fort Worth, Texas, and with Billy Cole in Des Moines, Iowa, over the radio.

Wherever you'd see Bobby, he'd be walking, for that's the only way he had of getting around. He walked to the home of his guardian every night, too, and there he was given two dollars for his next day's meals.

"Can't eat much for two dollars, though," Bobby said. "I can't afford to eat breakfast anymore."

Bobby's favorite supper spot was the Three Pigs Restaurant to which he walked from his rooming house on the other side of town every evening.

"Mary Abel gives me a plate on the house every night," he said. "She's that kind of a person."

Bobby felt that everyone in town was nice to him.

"Sometimes," he said realistically, "they get all crossed up, but," he added forgivingly, "I don't pay no attention to that. I know I'm always welcome around them."

Bobby said that he was "just partially" a member of the Church of Christ, and that he didn't curse, or smoke or drink anyway.

His worst hours were those that found him penniless, and it was then that he wished desperately that he might have a *Times-Mail* paper route.

But he consoled himself with the good fortune in his life — the room at Kate's, where he could crawl into bed at the end of the day, and sleep.

MOTHER'S DAY

I placed a violet on her grave. Just one.

I have no idea who she was, but she was a mother, as attested by the gray stone at the foot of her grave.

Chiseled into its sloping dappled face was the single word, "MOTHER."

Opposite the small stone was the moss-splotched base from which a larger stone once rose bearing her epitaph. But it was gone, the victim of time . . .? Vandals . . .?

The violet was growing nearby, almost underfoot, as I walked past the scaly, gray, abandoned remains of a church that humped from a thickening growth of unkept green grass.

When I found her grave I went back, pinched the flower's long stem close to the ground and carried it to her.

It lay there on the grave, its color a reflection of my mood.

"Happy Mother's Day," I whispered. And I wondered how many she had celebrated in her lifetime; how many children had come to her in her years and said, "Happy Mother's Day, Mother." I wondered if she could read my thoughts, if they aroused pleasant memories for her, and if she were smiling through misty eyes at the recollections.

Happy Mother's Day, Mother.

I tried to remember how many times I had expressed that sentiment in my lifetime, and I couldn't recall a single time.

I'm sure I did. Maybe I'll recall them another day.

Memories of other days came to mind; my First Holy Communion, when my widowed, immigrant mother stood with fingers entwined about a beading rosary, watching proudly as I walked to the altar in blue serge knickerbockers and starched white shirt; and I remembered ten of us children sitting around an oval table as she served food, coaxing, threatening, often weeping at our lack of appetite and appreciation; and the night she came to Town Hall where I, along with a group of boyhood confederates, was being held in the town jail for stealing fruit from an orchard on Campbell St.; and oh, the day Miss Quirk stopped at our small New England town home to tell her that I had been caught smoking in the little boy's room at school; and the day I came out from under an anesthetic of ether, a frightened boy, in Miriam Hospital, in Providence, far from home, and she was sitting by my bed, rosary again in hand, praying, waiting.

It seems that she was always praying and waiting – for us to return at the end of the day; for us to keep a promised appointment with her; to obey her; to come home safely at night; to join her at Mass; to demonstrate our love for her; for us to grow up, and later, for us to come home from our wars.

You could see the strain of waiting in her face as she prepared to go to daily Mass; you could hear it at night as she plodded through her clicking beads. My God, the trips she made around those five decades of Paters and Aves! Always praying. Always waiting. Waiting in a world, a life, as solitary and blue as the violet I had placed on the anonymous grave.

Had I ever said, "Happy Mother's Day, Mother?" I searched my memory again.

There had been so many frantic years. Yet I must have said it every Mother's Day . . .? I can't remember!

"I used to tip-toe behind her while she was standing at the coal-wood range, cooking, and hug her; just wrap my arms around her and squeeze, kiss her on the neck, and then turn and run," I said with my eyes on the violet.

I had to laugh at the memory, because it always startled her, and kind of embarrassed her, even though she knew, and I knew, that she liked it.

"Did your sons hug and squeeze you like that? Kiss you like that?" I said with my eyes searching the green grave beyond the violet. "Funny. I can't remember having done that on a Mother's Day though. It was always one of those spur of the moment things that are so hard to explain."

Is my memory so bad that I cannot remember a Mother's Day with her? I remember June 24, 1955! The memory of that day is as clear and sharp as the pealing of a bell. It began with the sound of a bell – a ringing telephone bell.

"She was even then being prepared for surgery," I stared the words into the sloping gray stone that replied only with a soundless, chiseled "MOTHER."

The days were few after that. And even though she knew better than we what was to take place on the approaching fourteenth day of September we couldn't allow the obviousness of too much affection – for her sake.

Yet we did; in song; in laughing recollection; in a bouquet of hand-picked wildflowers. We did show her much affection, and it did not weaken her, for I know now that she had known all her life – at least all the years I had known her – for what she had been waiting. And when her appointment was kept it was with grace and happiness which were as sincere as was the strength of her resolve. And her last thoughts, her last words, were for us.

"She's at rest far from here," I spoke to the ancient stone again. "I'd like to think you were like her, if you don't mind. Yes, I'd like to think that.

"And I'd like to think that your children were affectionate toward you; that at least one of them hugged and squeezed you and kissed you on the neck on at least one Mother's Day and said, 'Happy Mother's Day, Mother.' And I wish, too, that he can remember having done so – for his sake."

INDIAN AND TRINITY SPRINGS

They tell a story in Indian Springs about the first train ever to appear in the small Martin County community when it was a thriving sulphur springs resort, before the turn of the century.

Almost everyone from miles around was on hand to witness the great arrival. As the steam locomotive pulling the mail and passenger coaches chugged and clanged up to the new native timber platform and depot the crowd's cheers drowned out the sounds of its boiler and bell.

After the train came safely to a stop curious people climbed up on the platform and surrounded the impressive engine, tender and coaches. Dozens of passengers attempting to disembark to visit the sulphur springs found it almost impossible to escape the happy, celebrating throng.

Finally it was time for the train to depart, and to attract the noisy, pressing horde's attention, the engineer sounded a railroader's hi-ball – he tooted the engine's whistle sharply a couple of times.

Toot-toot!

The crowd was startled into silence.

"Now if you people will back away just a little," the engineer called out from the cab of the locomotive while motioning with a wave of his hand, "I believe I can turn this thing around."

57

It is said that near panic ensued as the hundreds of people there fell over one another in their anxiety to get out of the way.

"Of course," Arnold Hitchcock said to me in his home at Indian Springs, "that's a story that's been told and retold here about the coming of the railroad."

Another concerns William Jennings Bryan, three-time seeker of the presidency.

"My father told me he stayed here in his private railroad car," Hitchcock said.

But Hitchcock didn't know if the peerless leader of the Democrat party was in Indian Springs during the campaign of 1896, 1900 or 1908.

It was known that the Indiana Democratic Editors Association arrived in their own private railroad coach for a convention there in 1888. There was a marked difference in the Indian Springs of that period and the near-deserted Indian Springs I found on my first visit there.

Hitchcock, who sometimes spoke before civic and service clubs and other groups about the community's past, told of a time of bloom and growth in Indian Springs that was difficult to imagine from the evidence that greeted me there. The popularity of its sulphur water and springs as a treatment and cure for almost every ill and ailment once attracted hundreds. So lucrative was the growing town for investors that a hundred thousand dollar hotel of Indiana limestone was planned there before nearby Trinity Springs began beckoning the majority of seekers of sulphur water cures.

Trinity, in its turn, was to lose its popularity to French Lick and West Baden, but not before Indian Springs continued as a railroad center. It was the nearest rail depot to Trinity, and the hundreds of annual visitors to the sulphur springs there still arrived by train at Indian Springs.

"There were three livery stables here at one time,"

Hitchcock said. "All kinds of hacks loaded with people, going from here to Trinity and back to the railroad."

The railroad was no longer a part of the town when I visited Hitchcock at his home. Several years before that the depot had been removed, as was the platform, and high weeds covered the area where they had sat empty and idle for so many years. Paul Gee's father used to work in the depot as railroad agent and telegrapher before his death in 1927.

"He died of measles and pneumonia fever," Paul told me. "But," he said, "he worked there for twenty years before he died and left seven kids. He saw some of the good times here."

Paul, however, was a child at the time of Asa Gee's death, and he was never apprised of, nor could he chronicle, those salad days. Of his own time Paul remembered that the taller of the old buildings that once made up Della Dillon's broiler chicken house had been the former Indian Springs School which he had attended for eight grades. He recalled some of his teachers there: Gladys Lewis, Leston George, Ray Chandler and Clair Baker.

When Della built the broiler house years before, she simply added on to the old school house, which she had purchased. There was no school in Indian Springs at this time, nor was there much of anything else, except a fourth class post office where Mamie Sheetz, the postmaster, spent a few hours each morning serving twenty of the thirty families that lived there. Ten of the thirty received their mail on a Shoals motor route.

If Indian Springs did not live in the present it at least lived in the past, thanks to Hitchcock. He made it come alive with his tales of the way it was – the sulphur springs, the visitors, dressed rabbits for sale hanging from nails in front of the general store, the Cincinnati Reds playing ball there, distilleries making whiskey there, fresh oysters arriving by train, Pluto water bottled and shipped from there, and former Bedford Mayor Lovell Harp having been born there, and Paul Spoonmore.

Trinity Springs wasn't always, as someone once said, "In the middle of nothing on the edge of nowhere," nor was its population always only a handful of people as it was during this first visit. There was a time when it was in the mainstream of life, popular, and populated. Platted in 1837 as Harrisonville, it was named for William Henry (Tippecanoe) Harrison. By 1870 Harrisonville had been renamed, and was a thriving community with stores, industry, a school and several hotels. In 1900 George Ballard built a forty-five room hotel there which was purchased seventeen years later by J.W. Thompson. He enlarged the hotel, added several new features, including a lake for fishing, and a hundred tents for visitors in a grove adjoining the hotel.

Whatever the ailment – high blood pressure, arthritis, nervous stomach, low back pain – Trinity's sulphur springs in the 1800s were a publicly venerated cure. They attracted the ailing and the afflicted from near and far to drink and to bathe in the pungent sulphur water that even during my first visit still bubbled up from a mysterious source into a stream at the edge of the hamlet.

Bathing was enjoyed in the strong smelling water in three springs shaped by industrious men of another era in the form of pools, with stone pavilions rising from their edges. But not only the ailing and the afflicted went to Indian and Trinity springs. Many who sought weekend respite and pleasures from the monotony of everyday living, and those who wanted the excitement of new faces, new acquaintances, and those who looked only to turn a dollar at the gambling tables, also went there.

Proof of their having been there was chiseled in the limestone outcroppings above the springs, where some

60

left their names, and even their home addresses. While they were there they also left their dollars, and there were those who populated the hamlets then who were pleased to accept them. A few of those who went there – it is said – also left their ailments, but some left their hopes, and went home to die.

The discovery of mineral springs at French Lick and West Baden, and the construction in those communities of massive, posh hotels, surely brought about the demise of bustling Trinity, and what remained of Indian Springs as a resort. Whatever the cause. Trinity, much like Indian Springs, became sparsely populated. The large hotel which catered to visitors was hauled away piece by piece by souvenir hunters. The ailing and the afflicted returned no more. The stone floors of the popular curing springs became overgrown with green moss, and their abandoned waters filled with the fallen leaves and twigs of many years. The chiseled names in the limestone outcroppings, under the wear of treading seasons, were worn away until all that remained unchanged was the stench of the reputed healthful waters.

In recent years the Indiana State Highway Commission improved that part of State Road 450 which connects Trinity to Williams to the northeast and Dover Hill to the southwest. In the midst of the decay which began so long ago, that stretch of new blacktop with its eight-foot shoulders appeared shockingly anachronistic.

Somewhere in the eight-foot shoulders lay the ghosts of Cundiff's Restaurant, Brassine's Grocery Store, and the old iron bridge that I found on my first visit to Trinity. Their absence on my last visit there spoke loudly and clearly to me that the Trinity Springs of my first visit was also gone.

Despite that, visitors, I was told, still arrived there and at Indian Springs. If not for sulphur water, then out of curiosity, out of a fascination with what once was.

THE ROAD BUILDERS

Were a book of successful men and women in our time and place to be compiled, there might be an interesting entry under T for Thomas, W. L., Inc.; or , better, under T for Tuffy and Treva Thomas.

"Millionaires," it might honestly begin, and it could add, "in the most unlikely of places – Owensburg."

For clarification it might point out, "Heavy equipment operators and road builders."

Then the entry might include at least a thumb-nail sketch of the husband and wife team:

Willis Leo (Tuffy) Thomas was born in remote Dog Trot in Martin County, and attended the one-room school there before his widowed mother moved her family of seven two miles away to Owensburg in Greene County.

And it would continue: Treva Cobb Thomas, a girl who was raised in Owensburg by her maternal grandmother, Minnie Smith, grew up with Tuffy, went to school with him, and later dated him until their marriage, November 6, 1941.

"I was six when my father died," Tuffy drawled from a chair in the offices of W. L. Thomas, Inc., at Owensburg one day. "His name was Arthur Thomas, and he used to haul logs to the railhead at Indian Springs. One winter he accidentally froze his feet and he died from gangrene. When we moved here I finished school here, but I don't have an education. I'm just like mostly everybody else around here. We got what schooling was available and then we went to work."

Tuffy became a heavy equipment operator at eighteen, saved his money, bought a bulldozer and began doing custom work. Treva kept the books. They later launched the Triangle Construction Company, in Bedford, with partner George Sargent. In 1960 they sold out to Sargent and founded the company known as W. L. Thomas, Inc., in Owensburg.

"I couldn't have done it without Treva," Tuffy said of the succuss of W. L. Thomas Inc. "She had more faith in me than a government mule. That helps, believe me.

"We struggled for a long time, so far in debt that it would have scared an average person to death. Everything came the hard way. Treva was the one who kept me going, kept me trying. And we never missed a payment; we sure never did," he said.

Children of the Great Depression, when a piece of store-bought bread was a special taste treat and a banana was like manna, Tuffy and Treva had cut their teeth on tough times. Although they had the proverbial pot when they began their life together, they barely had a window out of which to throw it.

"We sold a 1941 Ford to get the money to buy three rooms with a pump outside and an outhouse," Treva remembered. "And we lived there for thirty-one years."

"It's not too bad to be broke when everyone else is," Tuffy remembered. "That's the way it used to be."

The Thomases live in a very comfortable red brick home of several rooms, much of which was built by Tuffy himself. A mansion compared to their first home, it is on a site of one hundred and fifteen lush acres and includes a six-acre blue water lake, built by Tuffy, and stables where several Thomas horses were kept. A large picture window in the home opens on a view of sheer beauty: the lake in the foreground, complete with waiting pontoon boat at a small dock and, under an agate blue sky, a sweep of manicured verdant acres in the background. On another two hundred and twenty acres the Thomases have a secluded cabin on the shore of a still larger lake.

"I love it all," Tuffy, a hunter-fisherman and nature lover, said. "You hack something out yourself and it means a whole lot more to you. I can travel to anyplace in the world if I want. I have been to Europe and Saudi Arabia. But I'd a whole lot rather just stay right here. We like it here, and," he said of the five children of his and Treva's two children, "we get an awful lot of fun out of our grandchildren and great-grandchildren."

A big, easy-going fellow whose calm and congeniality belie the struggles of the past, Tuffy, and the friendly Treva, once owned as many as fifty large road-building machines. In sharp contrast to those early days at Dog Trot and Owensburg, they relax atop a heap of dollars that number in millions.

"We've done real well, but if I had ten times more it wouldn't change me. I'm the same person that I ever was. I still want people to like me," Tuffy said.

When I inquired about it Tuffy explained his nickname.

"Our closest neighbor at Dog Trot had nine boys and they did everything imaginable to me," he replied. "They beat me, kicked me, swung me by the hair. You name it and they did it to me. And they began calling me Tuffy.

"The name stuck, and people have known me all my life by that name. I get mail in the name of Tuffy

Thomas, and many of our checks have been made out that way. The name follows me wherever I go, and people always ask how it came about."

It was during their travels that a most unusual thing happened to Tuffy. While riding as a passenger in an airline over the Yukon Territory he suffered a broken leg when the plane struck turbulance at thirty-five thousand feet.

"I was taken to a hospital in White Horse where they set my leg and gave me a pair of crutches, and they wouldn't take a penny in payment," Tuffy said. "That's the way they do in Canada."

Treva is a duplicate stamp of her husband's view of himself and of their home.

"I don't think of myself as being any different than I ever was," she said. "I'm still the same person. We still put out a garden every year. We still do a lot of canning, just like we always did, and Tuffy still mows the lawn. I'm not a big shopper, and I love my home. Like Tuffy, I'd rather be home in Owensburg than any place I know."

For years after they started their company Treva kept the books without the aid of an adding machine.

"I worked all day and sat up all night figuring accounts and bills until I got on to it," she said.

She is proud of a letter received from an IRS office about her work. In it she was complimented for keeping the "neatest set of books we've ever seen." There was not a single erasure in them.

A story about Tuffy and Treva would not be complete without mentioning their gravestone, set on a twelve-grave plot in the Owensburg Cemetery. Quarried in Vermont especially for them it is a huge block of gray granite two feet thick and five and one half feet high with concave and convex surfaces. It weighed twelve thousand pounds when it was shipped from the quarry and was set on a footer of seven yards of concrete. Carved into the smooth surface of one side is the symbol of Tuffy's and Treva's success, a D-8 Caterpillar bulldozer. Standing out in relief are large letters that spell THOMAS.

"I wanted something big and rugged," Tuffy said of the monument. "I had it done because I wanted to see it."

Also chiseled into the gray granite is a sentiment authored by Treva. It reads: "They built a road of love that others may follow."

At the time of this writing Tuffy and Treva were approaching their fifty-fourth wedding anniversary. Also at this time much of the responsibility of W. L. Thomas, Inc. was left to their son, Myron, and a grandson, Greg Todd. But, Tuffy remained very much on top of what was going on.

"I've slowed down," he conceded, "but I'm not retired. I don't ever want to retire."

THE SQUIRREL HUNTER

I was driving along Brummetts Creek Road to an interview when I saw her sitting on the swing. When I asked if I might visit with her she nodded her head toward the other side of the swing. She had beans to pick, she said, but she was waiting for the sun to dry the dew on the bushes. So she was kind enough to let me sit, and give me some time, and some advice to pass on to squirrel hunters.

"I'd just go out, slippin' along in the woods, and go to a hickory tree and sit down. When they go to comin', kill them."

Eva Stevens had raised a non-existent gun to her shoulder, aimed along a barrel that wasn't there, and ever so slightly squeezed the missing trigger as she explained her life-long method of hunting the little animals.

That's the way she always did it, she said, and that was the way she did it one year – "no, by golly, it was two years in a row" – when she bagged fifty-one that way, all by herself. And that, in any squirrel hunter's book, is a lot of squirrels.

"One year," she added, "the price of shells went up, and I said to myself, 'You're agoin' to have to take better aim,' and I killed fifteen that year with fifteen shots. I never missed a one."

The green slat swing on which we sat was suspended

67

by chains from a length of utility pole stretched horizontally from the fork of a one-hundred year old hard maple to the fork of another tree, another one-hundred year old hard maple. The cool breeze under the two tall, widespread trees was in sharp contrast to the unusual heat of the surrounding morning.

On her head Eva Stevens wore an aged straw hat with a ragged wide brim, and over her house dress she wore an old apron that fit up over her shoulders and tied in the back. In her right hand she held an old broomstick cane.

"I won't be agoin' huntin' this fall, and I didn't go last fall," she said. Then she tilted her head, touched a laced, bulky black shoe with the end of the broomstick, and she said, "I don't know if I could walk out to that big hickory." She nodded toward a large tree some distance away. "If I get in a big notion I might just light out."

Behind the lenses of harlequin frames her dark blue eyes glistened.

"Last thing I killed was a chicken hawk," she said. "I saw him flyin' over and I let him have it. He flopped his wings a li'l bit, and he flew over there," she pointed the broomstick across Brummetts Creek Road to a pasture where a small herd of red and white spotted cattle were feeding, "and he turned up his heels."

Eva Stevens nodded her head forward when she spoke the word "heels" to emphasize her enduring marksmanship and, as she did, her white hair shone silvery from under the back of the old straw hat.

She had come to the hundred eighty-two acres east of Bloomington from east of Unionville sixty-eight years earlier as the eighteen year old bride of Homer Stevens. It was Homer who had encouraged her to hunt, and together they hunted rabbit, quail, squirrel and possum, while also taking a toll on the groundhog and polecat populations.

As a young woman and long into her married life she had followed a walking plow, a cultivator, and she had done general farm work while her husband labored at a job in town so that they could "pay off the place," she said.

"I've swung many a mowin' scythe too," she said proudly, "and I put up my share of hay. But I did most of my work with horses. I don't care much about tractors they use today. I suppose I'm old fashion." She turned her head to look at me, her eyes still glistening. "You would be too," she said, "if you was eighty-five."

She remembered when people were sociable, and when they willingly helped one another without pay, and she compared herself to the change in too many people by saying disdainfully, "I never was a two-legged hog."

But she still had many good friends, she avowed, and they "fetched" her many good things to eat. Still, she was disheartened by the "some" who were selfish and untrustworthy.

"Seems like every feller is for himself, and you can't believe nobody anymore," she said. "I was always learnt to be what you are."

Being what she was set her apart from most, which she herself admitted, and without preamble she went on to express her view of "churchiness" with the same refreshing honesty.

"Church'll never save you," she said. Although she had attended several ("I wouldn't go to just one church."), and she sang in their choirs for thirty years, she expressed that honesty in this manner: "Why land o-rest! Only one way to be saved, and you do that in your daily walks. Daily walks is what talks."

She called my attention to her guineas and how they walked the garden rows and picked beetles off the beans and bugs and potatoes, and did not harm the plants, and that the only way – "just about" – you can tell the hens from the roosters was that, "The hen hollers 'potterack' and the rooster he just jabbers."

Comparing herself to modern women, she said, "I guess I'm one in a hunnerd. I played ball when I was a girl. Baseball. But I was never no hand to be on the galligahoot."

Galligahooting had brought about the downfall of many good old institutions she opined, and one of those was respect for the sick.

"Neighbors used to set up with the sick, until they died, if'n they had to," she said. "But nowadays people's kids won't do that."

Another institution fallen to galligahooting, she said, was respect for the dead.

"Very few people hurts themselves being upset for the dead. Most of them are glad they've gone," she pushed the end of her broomstick cane at the ground, as though to put a period after that statement.

A widow of twenty-six years, she had no regrets about how she'd spent her years, and she confessed that if she had them to live over she'd try to be a little better each day.

"But my land o-rest," she said, "I never went to bed hungry, and I never got rich."

On the ground to the right of the swing a metal bucket lay on its side. It was time to begin filling it with beans from one of her two gardens.

"Murderation no, I don't set on any stool when I pick beans," she snapped at my question as though sitting while she worked was a disgrace. "When I have to do that I'll go to crawlin' on my knees."

Returning to squirrel hunting, she said, "I don't have to go away from home to hunt when I've got a hunnerd and eighty-two acres here. I might hunt this fall, if I can walk out to that big hickory," she nodded in the direction of the big tree again. "I reckon it's kind of a lazy man's job – a heap more than rabbit huntin'."

Suddenly getting to her feet with bucket in hand she moved as sprightly and as certainly as a woman half her age.

"I've got beans to pick," she said, jabbing the broomstick cane into the earth. "And roastin' ears are ready to gather, and there'r potatoes to dig, and there's kraut to make . . ."

Without actually saying as much, Eva Stevens had terminated our morning visit.

THE TIN CAN MAN

It was only natural that I should have felt some concern when from my car I saw the man hanging half in and half out of the state recreation area dumpster. No, he wasn't dead, nor was he unconscious. He was very much alive and busy retrieving empty, cast-off aluminum soda and beer cans with a long stick. He'd poke with the stick, push its tapered point into the opening of a can, and flip it out of the dumpster. The method was a touch of genius, something to witness even from a distance.

But I was worried for his safety. More often than not there were hordes of bees in such dumpsters. They liked empty cans, or rather the dregs of soda and beer left in them. They also were known to sting people who interfered with their pleasure. It seemed that almost every time I'd taken trash to a dumpster I wound up a victim of bee stings. If I was not flailing my arms at one or more zooming around my head I was from a distance keeping an anxious eye on them buzzing around the place I needed to be.

I readily accept the fact that bees and I do not get on. Something about our chemistries, I think. My first experience with them came when I was a boy of seven or eight. I inadvertently walked into their territory, a shallow watery place, probably a drain of some kind. That was all the excuse they needed. I was stung several times on my hands and face. I ran home bawling from the pain and almost blinded by the swelling. My mother covered the stings with a thick paste of some kind and warned me to stay away from bees, which I've tried to do.

There was another time when I was talking to an acquaintance and two of those yellow pests crawled undisturbed over the fingers of one of her hands.

"Hey," I said worriedly, "there are a couple of bees crawling on your hand."

"I know," she said with startling indifference.

"They'll sting you," I cried out.

"No they won't," she said calmly.

They didn't.

A couple minutes later a bee whose attention was distracted by the shine of a ring of keys dangling from my left hand stung me on the finger.

"How about that?" I demanded angrily.

"Oh, you probably moved," my friend said.

"Of course I moved," I shouted. "I move every time a bee lights on me. What else do you expect me to do, stand there and get stung?"

"You're not supposed to move," she said.

"You're not supposed to be running loose," I retorted.

So this guy, naked to the waist, was hanging half in and half out of the dumpster with bees all around him. I drove over and stopped and rolled down the car window, feeling the summer's heat rush into my air-conditioned cubicle as I did so.

"Hey," I called to him. "Aren't you afraid of those bees? You know they'll sting you, don't you?"

He gave me a big smile that was without a sign of a single tooth in it. If you are not already aware of it, I'll tell you, there is no smile bigger and deeper and more meaningful than one with no teeth in it. Next time you

73

see one check it out. You'll note that it is not narrow and shallow or otherwise obscured by one or more rows of teeth. You'll note that it is big and wide and deep, and innocent and harmless, and as winning as a new-born baby's smile. A smile like that always gets to me and I liked the guy right off.

"They won't bother me," he said assuringly.

"That's what you think. They'll get you," I warned.

"Naw, not me," he said. "I talk to them."

"You what?" I asked.

"I talk to them," he repeated, still smiling that friendly cavernous smile. "I talk bee talk to them."

This is the truth, so help me.

So I told him, "It won't work, Buddy. Take it from me, I tried talking bee talk to bees one day and it didn't work."

"You didn't talk right," this guy said with what sounded like a tone of authority in his voice.

"Yes I did," I argued. "I was mowing my lawn and a whole bunch of those yellow devils came up out of the ground and stung me on the back of my legs . . ."

"You should have talked bee talk to them," he interrupted me.

"I did," I said defiantly. "I danced around the yard waving my arms and hollering, 'Buzz off you son of a bee! Buzz off you son of a bee!' and Mister, I might just as well have been talking to the lawn mower. They just kept working me over till I made it to the house and shut the screen door behind me."

His smile seemed wider and deeper than ever.

"Aw," he said, "you're just funnin' about that."

"So help me, Mister," I told him, "if every word I just spoke isn't the truth I hope one of those bees in that dumpster comes over here and stings me."

Then I hurriedly rolled up my car window and drove away from there. Not because I hadn't told the truth.

74

I was just afraid that one of those sons of bees might just try to make me look like a liar.

Because the state recreation area was near enough to my home that I could do so without much effort, I had been stopping there almost every day to walk for my health. While I was involved in such a session a few days later, I ran into the man again. We were nowhere near a dumpster, and there were no bees around, so I decided to learn what I could about him.

He was unemployed, and because he collected aluminum cans to help support himself some people called him "The Tin Can Man." That was an okay handle with him, and it was with me, too. I told him at the outset of our talk he might become a newspaper column subject for me and that also was okay with him. However, he told me he had five married children and he preferred they didn't know how he eked out his living. He said he saw them only occasionally because they lived away from Bloomington. When on rare meetings with him they wanted to know how he was doing, he said he told them, "I eat well, and I'm getting plenty of exercise."

That seemed to satisfy them. They were unaware that his only shelter was a pup-tent in the campground of the state recreation area. They knew nothing about how each night he placed two folded blankets under his sleeping bag to protect him from the hard, damp ground. And they might have been surprised to learn he cooked and ate under whatever skies nature provided.

Judging from his demeanor, however, and some remarks he made, they might not have cared. Seems something had been lost between them long before I met him. They'd had a home together for eighteen years, during his one and only marriage. Life was different then. Better. But because he had a special need, as he called it, there was trouble, then a divorce, and things went from bad to worse for him.

In as few words as possible this is what happened: He had been a salesman, a good one, he said, but on the road. Blinded by his work, and his special need, he was unable to see that his marriage was falling apart, his family too. One day he sobered up and they were gone; they just weren't there anymore.

It was a long and bitter tumble from being on top to becoming one of the anonymous homeless and unemployed. He couldn't have done it by himself. He couldn't have done it without his special need. He knew that. In his case it took a good deal of his special need to sustain the plunge, but he finally made it. And when we met he was at the bottom of it, rueful, penitent, collecting aluminum cans from dumpsters and ditches, and walking ten miles a day to make his rounds.

He calculated his earnings in different ways. He told me it took twenty-five cans to earn sixty cents. A large plastic trash bag held approximately sixteen pounds of cans. They converted to roughly ten dollars at the junkyard, but only when he could find transportation, for he had no car, no truck.

Thanks to a thirsty vacationing public during a three day Memorial weekend, he was able to collect one hundred sixty-four pounds of cans to earn himself one hundred thirteen dollars. The ensuing three-day Fourth of July weekend collections brought him ninety-five dollars, and the subsequent Labor Day weekend only sixty-four dollars.

To supplement his weekly earnings from the cans, he sold blood plasma two times a week. He received ten dollars for the first visit and fifteen dollars for the second. According to his figures the cans and the plasma provided him with an average weekly summer income of about eighty dollars.

In spite of the way he lived, there were expenses. The pup-tent cost twenty-eight dollars. And because he ate well, food was not a small item. Availing himself of the recreation area's facilities he kept himself neat and clean, and soaps and other toiletries took some of his money. He was a weekly visitor to a coin laundry. To stretch his dollars he bought what clothes he had to have at a thrift store.

There were emergency expenses too. Strong winds one night destroyed a pup-tent and he was forced to buy another. He also had to do something about his less than 20/20 vision; he spent fourteen dollars for a pair of drugstore magnifying eyeglasses. He said he'd been looking for a job – one in sales. But he added that no one wanted him because of his toothless appearance.

"I worked from 1950 to 1980," he told me. "I worked in a factory once. But I worked as a salesman most of the time. I was considered successful. Now nobody wants me because I have no teeth.

"Just the other day a fellow said I could come to work for him, selling cars. He said, 'You can come in Monday, but bring your teeth with you.'

"That hurts your feelings," The Tin Can Man appeared deeply saddened. "I don't have any teeth. But I can hold my mouth in such a way when I talk so's you can't tell."

He proceeded to form his mouth a certain way, the movement seemingly making a line of his mouth that accented his jutting chin. It was anybody's guess from his appearance then if he did or did not have teeth.

"And I can sell," he continued, and it became quickly obvious when he spoke that he did not have any teeth in his mouth. "So why not hire me now? A set of teeth costs two hundred dollars at the dental school at Indiana University. I don't have that kind of money.

Not now. But I'm saving it. I've got a good education. I played basketball in the seventh and eighth grades at Mitchell.

"I was a freshman at University High School, in Bloomington, and I graduated from Warren Central at Indianapolis. I'd have played basketball for Branch McCracken, at Indiana, but I wasn't tall enough."

He stood an even six-feet. The summer regimen of ten miles a day had brought his weight down twenty pounds, to a hundred and ninety-eight. He hadn't smoked for thirty-five years and he said he didn't drink anymore. He also was very likeable.

Still, discouragement comes easy for guys like him and in the throes of it he was inclined to project his thoughts into the future. He looked forward to his sixty-second birthday when he would be eligible to receive a monthly Social Security stipend. Then maybe he might live better, he said.

But that was still five years out the road. Between him and then was the immediate promise of cold weather. Will it be a job for him, he wondered, or will it be a room in a mission home in Louisville, Kentucky, where he'd spent the previous winter? He said he was hoping someone would give him a job.

He did have a job of sorts. He had found a sympathetic listener in the lady who leased the campground general store concession from the Indiana Department of Natural Resources, and she let him do a little work around the place for her. She paid him in cash and food. Being a kindly person and ready listener she also gave him moral and spiritual support. She was probably one of the best friends he ever had.

I included his hope for a job in a Sunday column about him, and, as we had agreed, I referred to him only as The Tin Can Man. Before that morning was over the doorbell at our house sounded. When I answered, it was to find a big, kindly Hoosier with a drawl as rich and smooth as home-churned butter standing there. Without fanfare he announced that he had a job for The Tin Can Man, if he was interested.

It was one of those made-to-order deals, one of those dreamed-about offers, that comes along once in a blue moon. The job, if The Tin Can Man could handle it, was to care for the big man's elderly father in exchange for bed and board, a small salary, and Sundays off.

I couldn't answer for The Tin Can Man, neither did I care to embarrass him further by exposing his living conditions to a stranger. So with my heart beating a little faster than normal I drove to the state recreation area to inform The Tin Can Man of my morning visitor. He got excited about the offer. I arranged a meeting at which the big man who had called at my house explained his proposition in detail. The Tin Can Man accepted. The big man said he would pick him up the next day and take him and his pup-tent and his sleeping bag and blankets home with him.

Thrilled at his good fortune, The Tin Can Man that night lay sleepless in his pup-tent. He kept telling himself that what had happened to him was just too good to be true. He tossed and turned fitfully. Finally he got up and went outside where he sat at one of those state recreation area picnic tables. And in the glow of a campground electric light he made some notes on lined tablet paper.

"One more night and I'll be out of my tent and into a modern home," he wrote. "No more cooking out, sleeping on the ground and using outhouses. I'll be washing my clothes in an automatic washer instead of a five gallon bucket. I'll be riding in a van, a Buick, or Ford pickup, instead of walking or hiring a ride. I'll be cooking on an electric stove, and I'll have electric lights, and a refrigerator instead of a cooler. Tomorrow at four p.m. I'll be heading for my new home. And I'm ready. I'll soon be closer to heaven."

While it wouldn't be quite necessary for him to pass through the eye of a needle to get closer to his vision of heaven, The Tin Can Man would undergo a trial that night.

"The rain started suddenly," he wrote. "Just pouring down. And the wind was whipping the tent all around (He seemed inclined to writing in verse). As I lay in my tent on the cold, damp ground, thanking God for the home I had finally found, the two front straps that keep the rain out were jerked from my hands and sent all about."

When the blow subsided a half hour later he was soaked. Everything he owned was sopping wet, except his sleeping bag. It had somehow survived the wind-lashed downpour. Wet and cold, he zipped himself up in it and sat at the picnic table to await the dawn.

"I made it through the night," he wrote. "All I could say was 'Thanks a lot.'"

As promised, his benefactor arrived at four o'clock that day and The Tin Can Man went home. One evening a few weeks later they appeared at our front door. The Tin Can Man was radiant, pleased with his new situation. A roof over his head, his own bed in his own room, an elderly healthy, pleasant, considerate gentleman in his care, and a small bank account. He was satisfied, he said. He'd taped some verses he wanted me to hear, and some songs (I was not aware he could sing). He was happy. The big man also expressed his own satisfaction and pleasure at the success of the arrangement.

Here are a few words from the Tin Can Man's tape: "I have been very happy, and all is just fine. I only work about three hours a day, but I get room and board, and even some pay. My new employers are not only my friends, they are more like family. They will always have my gratitude. I have a new watch, new jeans, and money in the bank."

The Tin Can Man and his new employers also worked together around the property, shopped together, and went to church together. One day I answered our doorbell to find The Tin Can Man standing there. He greeted me with a big smile – no words – and for a few moments the silent message was unclear. Then it hit me. The usual gaping fullness of his smile was obscured by two rows of brand new, sparkling white teeth. What a surprise! He appeared actually handsome.

Some months later my wife and I drove to where The Tin Can Man had been given refuge. Simply put, he looked good. He was still satisfied, perhaps more than before, and he seemed happy. At one point during our conversation he said that the elderly man for whom he was caring was becoming like a father to him. I was moved. He also informed me that his benefactor had kindly been providing him with a weekly six-pack of beer. He could handle that, he said. No problem. It sounded so – all right, so innocent, so decent. On the drive home my wife and I discussed the man's good fortune at length, and we both thanked God for people like The Tin Can Man's benefactor and the nice things that were happening to him – well, to all of them.

A few years passed and when I decided to compile this book and title it "The Tin Can Man," I wanted to write a fitting end to this story, and one day my wife and I returned to where The Tin Can Man lived. We were met at the door by strangers who knew nothing of the man I sought, nor did they know anything about what I asked, except that the former resident was dead.

The Tin Can Man's benefactor who still lived next door was not at home. We drove around the small rural town and made some inquiries and soon we found The Tin Can Man's new quarters: a small battered camping trailer in high weeds near a barn wall at the edge of town, a canted wooden chair propped against its door holding it shut.

My world began turning gray. Something unpleasant has happened here, I said to myself. But what? Did I really want to know? We passed some hours waiting for The Tin Can Man to come home. He didn't, but the people who had been so good to him arrived home in late afternoon. From them we learned The Tin Can Man had been a good servant, almost like family and, until death had intervened, faithful and loyal to the needs of his patient day and night. In his spare time he chopped firewood. With the help of his benefactor he would sell it by the pickup truckload, some of it to the lady who ran the campground store at the state recreation area where this story began. Before long the Tin Can Man had a fair bank account.

"Then he wanted to buy a pickup truck of his own," his benefactor recounted. "I wasn't too sure that was the right thing to do, but it was his money. And we found a pickup for him."

Wheels gave The Tin Can Man a degree of independence for which he was ill-prepared. Wheels easily took him to the area taverns. Suddenly the six-pack of beer provided him weekly was not enough. His special need of earlier years began making the same old demand on him again, and he did not deny it.

"He stayed with my father for as long as my father lived, three years, I'll give him credit for that," his benefactor said. "And he was right there with him when my father died. After that he wanted to be out on his own. He was arrested for driving under the influence and his license was suspended. He rides a bicycle now."

On the ride home my wife and I said little, too steeped in our own thoughts. A few months went by and out driving one summer day I turned toward the town where The Tin Can Man lived. I was surprised to find him home, seated in a cast-off recliner in an outdoor living room he'd arranged near his camper under one corner of the tractor shelter of the old barn. He was naked to the waist and sipping from a can of beer.

"People give me their old furniture," he gestured to the chairs he had arranged on a clean square of carpet. "Sometimes they come to visit."

He looked well, even younger than his years. He told me that after leaving the employ of his benefactor he had worked for other people, caring for their aged or their sick. People liked him and had paid him generously, he said; and some had also provided him with living quarters. In time he had become eligible for Social Security and had quit working. He was retired, he said.

When I asked about his driver's license suspension he readily admitted that on more than one occasion he'd been picked up for drunk driving. But, he assured me, he wasn't drinking that much anymore. He had cut himself back to only one six-pack of beer a day, and he was able to handle that, he said.

ANNA (TOBY) NELSON

We were seated on the back porch of Freedom House situated on the west bank of the West Fork of White River at Freedom, and Toby Nelson was recalling another time in that place.

"I learned to swim in that river," she began. "I learned to row a boat in it, and I used to put my throw-lines out there and catch fish. I had a live-box there, too, and the boys from town used to come down and steal my fish out of it."

Anna G. (Toby) Nelson was one of those rare persons who in the twilight years of life was still rooted to the place where she was born and reared, and who could take from that knowledge, and her familiar surroundings, a pleasure unknown to so many of us. And when she said, "The word 'home' means a lot to me," there was no question about it.

Freedom House was the home of her parents, Fred and Hattie Fulk Nelson, whose produce enterprise of earlier years stretched from Worthington, just down the road in Indiana, to Memphis down in Tennessee.

In her early years, Toby attended the commissioned school at Freedom and then went on to nursing school at Methodist Hospital in Indianapolis. In 1925 she became administrator of the thirty-five bed Bloomington Hospital, and she continued in that position until her retirement in the spring of 1960.

Briefly reviewing those years as we did, and thinking about them and writing about them, was a whole lot easier than putting them together a day at a time, as Toby had done. She indicated as much in her answer to my question why she retired after thirty-five years. She said simply, "For me it was a twenty-four hour a day job; long hard hours. I retired because I was just worn out."

In those years she witnessed the hospital increase in size from thirty-five to fifty beds, and then to one hundred beds. And she employed a memory of the Great Depression to accent the difficulty that accompanied that storied growth.

"There was no money," she recalled. "Patients couldn't pay their bills, and we had to operate; had to have the hospital. So I had the nurses turn back half their salary to me, to help pay our expenses. It was hell, believe me. You try to take a hospital through a depression and you've got something on your hands."

She paused looking up-river to the suspension bridge, and the pre-stressed concrete extension of it where once had stood a covered bridge. Then she said, "The time came when I could repay all those wonderful people, and they were repaid."

Freedom, which is on State Road 67, is about nine miles down-river from Spencer. Just how many times Toby drove her car through that town on her way from Freedom House and Bloomington Hospital and back, over that roadway, probably will never be known. Although she sometimes thought she remembered them all, one of those drives stood out from the rest.

It was seven o'clock on a morning in February in 1955, and Toby was driving from the hospital home to Freedom House. A short distance west of Ellettsville an eastbound automobile suddenly veered over the center line and struck her car head-on.

How she survived the crash was always cause for

wonder; Toby's car was demolished. She lay in shock in her own hospital for ten days before her physicians dared treat her for her injuries. Her recovery lasted for months, and toward its end, during the better days of it, Toby had her bed moved into her office, where she could continue her job, overseeing the growing hospital.

The car that struck hers was a borrowed one. Its owner carried no insurance. Its drunk driver survived the violent crash without injury. Years later he would be shot fatally in a domestic quarrel, and a few years after that Toby would learn of it.

She smiled wryly at the memory of the belated information: "It wasn't done soon enough for me," she said. "It was a little late as far as I was concerned. I really got clobbered in that wreck."

She soon put the near-fatal experience back into the past, and she laughed, "We've got to train ourselves to remember the good times and not the bad," she said.

Among the good times was Christmas of that long and painful year. Toby, whose broken bones were still mending, and who was ambulatory only with the aid of a walker, faced a bleak Christmas at Freedom House without a tree unless someone came to her aid.

Someone did. Nurses Hollis LaBaw, Evelyn Lanam, Normal Roper, Peg Siscoe, Edna Reese, Dorothy Wray and Irene Kirkpatrick gathered at Freedom House and participated in the first of what became a traditional annual tree-trimming ceremony there.

When Toby lay near death after the auto accident those same nurses had volunteered their services and remained at her bedside around the clock until she was well enough to resume her administrative duties.

"They come here for my birthday, and they come here for Christmas, " Toby said fondly. Then she added, "They're super RNs."

A long window separated the back porch of Freedom

House from a comfortable living room that looked out on the river, the bridge up-stream and the greens of summer that climbed the opposite bank. Ten acres surrounded the beautiful home, and lawns, and flowers abounded there. A front porch, a back porch, a greenhouse and a guest house were welcoming and inviting.

Inside a long living room, untouched since Toby's mother decorated it years earlier, cherry drop-leaf tables and cherry corner cupboards and comfortable overstuffs and hanging Bessires and Loops and LaChances lent Freedom House an additional charm. The pleasure from all this almost became an ache and I yearned to see an autumn on the river from that long window, and a winter . . . a spring.

"We came home to Freedom House to live – and let live – in peace, and quiet," Toby said of the retirement she and Hollis shared there. "This is where I was born. This is the only home I've ever known. I'm deeply rooted here."

Hollis summed up what Toby said in a few words. "Toby," she declared, "is Freedom-born and Freedom-bound."

A MORNING'S WORK

Reading the jokes on a paper cocktail napkin over a sandwich and Coke in Jigg's and Jo's in Bloomfield may not have been some people's idea of work after a three week vacation, but I guess I was just unlucky. Yet, that's what I was doing – working.

"Mary had a bathing suit," I read the first joke which began in bright red print. "The latest style, no doubt. But when she got into it, she was half wayout!"

My thoughts went back a few days to some vacation hours. There had been several Marys in bathing suits on a beach – and some were more than half wayout. I remembered, too, that I had virtuously turned my head from them. Virtue? Green letters of the second joke before me on the tiny napkin danced with glee. "By the time men learn to behave themselves," I halted then long enough to make out their message, "they're too old for anything else."

And I thought I was being good these many years, I mused. Sonuvagun! Age must've sneaked up on me. And I wondered, do I like this, what's happened to me? I replied to myself, so what if I don't, where's the complaint department? I folded the napkin and slipped it into my shirt pocket – my daily work file, everything important went there. The dozen or so remaining jokes on the napkin would have to wait until I emptied the pocket on my dresser top that night. And I turned the rest of my lunchtime thoughts to a glorious hibiscus I'd seen earlier in the day, and a lady named Mary Ausman.

I was driving out North Road on my way to Brian Beuhler's Lucky Dollar Store, in Lyons, hoping I'd find a cardboard box there large enough to hold a litter of five puppies when I spied the hibiscus at the Ausman place. My boss might have shaken his head no-no had he known that he was financing my search for a cardboard box large enough to hold a litter of five puppies. The puppies? Well, let me also tell you about them.

Jimmy Reed, a nine year old, and his brother, Jason, who was seven, and Mike Korn, another nine year old, had been pumping their bicycles along North Road when they came across the abandoned litter. There never were three more excited boys, I'll tell you. The puppies were pretty excited too.

When the youngsters each held one to show them to me the puppies' heads stuck out at the top and their hind feet and tiny tails hung out at the bottom of their little hands. The other two puppies had been moved by bicycle to a secluded place amid a patch of tall weeds nearer to town, and the boys had come back for them when I happened along in my minitruck.

Of course I volunteered my services. It would have been a danger to life and limb to have allowed the transfer to continue as I found it. My mission clear, and agreed to by the four of us, I struck out for the Lucky Dollar Store. When I happened to see the beautiful pink hibiscus (at that time I knew only that the blooms were pink, beautiful, exotic, and not that they were beautiful pink hibiscus) I made up my mind to return and inquire about them.

After a caring girl at the Lucky Dollar Store named Billie went to a lot of trouble to find a box large enough to accommodate five little puppies I decided that I should also try to obtain one of those beautiful blooms for her. But we never seem to follow through on our nicest thoughts about people, do we? And Billie's kindness that day eventually went unrewarded.

Jimmy Reed, Mike Horn, Jason Reed

Meanwhile, back on North Road three little boys anxiously awaited my return while in their arms three hungry little puppies snuggled and pawed three soiled T-shirts in a hopeless search for ninny. By this time, too, the boys were either clearer in their account of the discovery of the litter or I was now listening with both ears. They'd found the puppies the previous evening, they told me. After transporting two of them to a safe place nearer to town, they had to go home – Mike's home; Jimmy and Jason, his cousins, were spending the night – to get ready for Sunday night church.

"Mom said we couldn't have them," Mike confessed.

90

"Not even two of them (now I knew why they had moved two and not three puppies). So we had to leave them in the weeds."

To their credit, despite the ultimatum delivered by Mike's mother, Darlene Woods, the boys did not have the heart to forsake the little animals. They had returned to North Road the next day, the day I met them, to secretly also move the other three puppies to the weed patch closer to town. From there they planned to inch them covertly toward the Woods home. They had heard Mike's stepdad, Rick Woods, say once that he wanted a pet dog, anyway. And they had high hopes that he might settle for five pet puppies instead.

"But Rick said 'one'," Darlene Woods almost moaned in her dismay at the sight of all of us — five hungry yipping puppies, three noisy little boys, and a gray-haired old stranger in a faded orange Datsun mini-truck — there in the Woods driveway. "I don't know what he'll say about five."

"Don't worry," I offered hopefully. "I'll put an ad in the paper along with your phone number. I'm sure there'll be all kinds of takers for these puppies."

Mike, her son, clasped a tiny black puppy to his little chest. There would be no taking from him. Jimmy and Jason held tiny puppies in their arms and hoped aloud their parents, Jack and Susan Reed (Susan and Darlene, I learned, were sisters) would allow them to keep theirs.

After having brought all that trouble to her house I considered myself lucky that Mike's mom hadn't clobbered me with a rock or something. But I got away unscathed and went back to North Road and the Ausman home. Mary Ausman came to the door in answer to my knock and we exchanged greetings and introductions. We talked for a while during which time I told her about my earlier puppy escapade.

Finally I asked her about the bush on which the large pink flowers bloomed.

"I don't know," Mary said. "I've forgotten the name. I got the bush out of a seed catalog years ago. And I just can't remember."

"Mind if I take a picture?" I asked.

"Go right ahead," she said.

During the process I noticed that the blooms were almost cone-shaped with four large petals that opened from a yellow center into a lovely delicate flower. It wasn't until I returned to the newspaper office that the bloom was identified. Hearing my description of it, secretary Linda Breeden spoke out: "Hibiscus," she said. Although a color photo in the World Book Encyclopedia did not support that identification, Linda's word was good enough for me. Hibiscus it was.

Anyway, the picture-taking at the Ausman place finished, Mary stood barefoot on the porch and talked to me about chicken, turkeys and guineas she kept there on North Road. When it suddenly dawned on her that I was a traveling newspaper reporter and that I might write about her flower, and her, she clammed up, but not before she had a few choice words for me.

"Be careful what you write about me," she said with a tight smile that was a warning in itself. "Or you'll find yourself in more hot water than you did when you took those puppies over to Darlene's."

I'd put down a delicious barbecue and two Cokes by the time I'd finished these reminiscences in Jigg's and Jo's and it was time to leave the restaurant. I paid up and let myself out the door. It was then that I noticed the sign overhead. It read, "The Spot." Not Jigg's and Jo's, as I had thought. Oh well, I sighed to myself, I'd worked too hard that morning to fret about it.

THE FLY

This story was told to me as the truth, but I have my doubts about it. Yet, they say that truth is sometimes stranger than fiction. No matter. If it will help you forget your troubles for a few minutes it'll be worth the telling. So sit back, relax and enjoy how a fly was credited with saving a marriage.

A young couple were having problems. It was one of those little things that too often tend to get dangerously out of hand and almost impossible to explain or rectify. So we won't worry ourselves with what it was all about because they themselves have difficulty remembering.

Still, the situation at the time had become precarious and they had not spoken for days. They shared the same house, ate at the same table, used the same conveniences, slept in the same bed, and yet they were so angry with each other they were thinking seriously to themselves of a separation.

Of course with the benefit of hindsight it all sounded silly to them later. But in the throes of selfishness, anger and argument, and the two of them working to make financial ends meet, well, their world was on the verge of falling apart.

Then one morning as she was dressing to go to her job, the zipper in her dress got stuck. Since it was in the back, and it had got stuck halfway between her waist and neck, she was unable to slip out of the garment and free the thing. She had to have help. Swallowing her pride she called out to her husband.

93

Without a word he went to her assistance and, standing behind her, pulled and tugged at the zipper rider until it came free. Then he allowed the devil to take hold of him. He grasped the zipper rider tightly in his fingers and zipped it up then zipped it down. He zipped it up again and down again, then up and down, up and down, as fast as he could, just trying to be funny yet releasing days of quiet anger and frustration while doing so.

Before she could stop him, or say anything – good or bad, the zipper broke, and he finally had to cut her out of the dress. She was enraged. It was an almost new garment. She had worn it only a few times. Now the zipper was torn out of it – it was ruined.

Moreover, all the accessories she planned to wear that morning had been carefully selected and laid out the previous night with that dress in mind. What was she going to do? For one thing she would be late to her job because she'd have to change, and it was his fault. She raged on and on, venting her pent-up emotions of the past few days.

She did arrive late at her job. For the rest of the morning she seethed about the ruined dress. She was so upset she could hardly do her work. At lunchtime she could barely eat half the sandwich she had ordered from the office deli.

She would get even. But try as she would, short of divorce she could not think of a way. The hours dragged by, and she could think of little else. So engrossed was she with revenge she seemed aloof to her co-workers. Thinking she might be ill they were kind and offered to help her with her work. She snarled at them and they withdrew, hurt and confused. Her mere presence in that rotten mood weighed heavily on everybody, and everybody was happy when quitting time came.

Driving home she was still seething; she was determined to have a showdown when she got there. She would put an end to the marriage. She'd show her husband. The more she thought about it the angrier she got. When she turned into her driveway her husband's car was already there. As she walked along the drive toward the house she saw two jeans-clad legs sticking out from under it. She assumed he was making some kind of repair. The misery of that whole day hit her like a lightning bolt. This, she told herself, was her great, and probably only opportunity to get even. And she became like putty in the hands of temptation.

She bent over and roughly grabbed the zipper in the jeans and zipped it down – then up, then she zipped it down again, and up again, then down and up, and down and up, so fast, so furiously, she lost count of the number of times. Then she dashed for the house.

Inside she froze, mouth hanging open; her husband was seated at the kitchen table drinking a cup of coffee. She felt ill. She thought she might faint. She sat down.

"What are you doing here?" she squeaked.

"I live here," he replied gruffly.

"Who's out there under your car? Whose . . ." she was almost screaming.

"Joe. The mechanic from the filling station," her husband said calmly. "Why?"

She was suddenly so embarrassed she barely had enough nerve to tell him what she'd done.

They rushed outside and called to the man still under the car. "Joe," shouted the husband. No response. "Joe," squeaked the embarrassed wife. Still no response. Together they grabbed Joe's legs and pulled him out from under the car. He was bleeding from a gash on his forehead and knocked out colder than a frozen mackerel.

The wife ran into the house and returned with some cold water and a washcloth. They sprinkled water on Joe's face and dabbed at the wound on his forehead with the wet cloth. He groaned a few times and came to.

"What happened?" asked the husband.

"I'm not sure," Joe groaned. "All I know is that I was under your car and something grabbed my fly."

The husband and wife hurried to explain and to express their mutual regret and sorrow at his pain and discomfort. It was their first act of togetherness in days.

95

Together they continued to help Joe, to make him comfortable. When he could stand they helped him home. As they prepared for bed that night they got talking about Joe and what had happened to him.

They said things such as, "I wonder what Joe thought was happening when you grabbed his fly," and, "I'll bet he got the surprise of his life," and, "I can just see him crunching his head under the car. Ouch!"

Despite poor Joe's pain and suffering the more they talked about the incident the funnier it became. They got tickled. Then they started laughing. They laughed and laughed and laughed until the tears came. Exhausted they fell on the bed hugging and kissing – their argument forgotten, and back in love again.

TREASURE OF DUTCH RIDGE

It was not so long ago that a pig in rural southcentral Indiana was worth no more than four plugs of chewing tobacco, and it wasn't a pig in a poke, either. It was an honest to goodness naked, squealy, smelly young pig with no strings attached, unless it would have been one man's addiction to tobacco and a general shortage of cash money.

It was a time in local history when a dollar was worth one hundred pennies, and precious few of those were around. It was a time when forest lands that now abound on both sides of State Road 446 in Monroe County were acres of mere seedlings. People in the surrounding hills and hollows were desperate for work, and they were hired for pennies a day by the "guv'mint" to stick the tiny plants into the ground.

On a bright summer's day, where the tall, straight pines now grow almost as thickly as hair on a dog's back, you will, if you listen closely, hear their ghosts as they come down from the slopes and up from the valleys.

If you watch closely you will see them as they were, dressed in washed-out, patched overalls, feed-sack dresses, and wearing ragged straws and faded bonnets on their heads.

You'll see them arched in the blistering sun, pushing the seedling pines into the ground, for hours on end seeing only the red clay on which they labored. They are the ghosts of less than a lifetime away, and if you peer closely you might see a familiar face, maybe two.

You will see, too, the dusty gravel roads that wound past the communities from which they came: Chapel Hill, Hunter Creek, Goat Run, Axsom Branch, Dutch Ridge and others.

Once bare and remote it is now a forest primeval lush with pine and redbud and dogwood, and abundant with strangers who travel from miles around to hunt the woodlands and fish and play in the guv'mint made reservoir at their center.

Enchanted by the names they find there, Sycamore Flats, Cutright Bridge, Bluegill Ridge, Southern Point and others, they wonder at the past, the homes that stood there, and those who lived and loved in them.

It was in that place that the value of a pig once was measured in plugs of chewing tobacco. It was a bargain perhaps equaled numerous times among those early people. I know of one, a swap made between one of them and the operator of a country store on wheels.

I was reminded of it when on a drive through Heltonville one day I saw Mack Todd installing an old school bell atop a family name sign in his front yard. Mack was the driver of the country store on wheels – a huckster wagon.

He was co-owner with Ray Bodenhamer of The Thrift Mart, a grocery store which was situated in the mid-1940s at the east edge of Bedford, on 16th St. His part of the partnership included driving the grocery on wheels to the Hickory Grove, Henderson Creek, Mundell, Zelma, Chapel Hill, Dutch Ridge and other rural neighborhoods.

The huckster wagon was a converted Chevy school bus whose inside was crammed with staples, twenty-four-pound bags of flour, one hundred pound sacks of sugar, and all manner of groceries and sundry items stacked on shelves. Lashed on a rack attached to the rear of the bus were a collection of chicken coops and a huge drum of kerosene for rural lamps.

World War II was a year or so in the past. Mack, a veteran of the Air Force, had flown an incredible number of bombing missions as a B-17 flight engineer over Germany, Austria, Yugoslavia, and northern Italy. Huckstering was probably his first peacetime effort on the way to better things.

"People always traded eggs and chickens for staples," Mack began recalling his experiences on that job as we talked in his front yard. "But this one day a man was waiting for me with a pig, and he asked to trade it for four plugs of Apple Chewing Tobacco. I accepted."

The trade was just that simple. Mack took the pig, the man took his chewing. After the transaction Mack put the big yellow bus in gear and drove off.

"I went on down the road with that pig loose in the bus," he remembered with a laugh. "He stayed with me until I found a fellow who offered me fifty cents for it. That wasn't a bad deal. The chewing tobacco sold for eight cents a plug, so I made a pretty good profit."

I wrote a column about our front-yard visit, and among other things I quoted Mack as saying, "There were a lot of good people on the routes." He recalled some of the names: "Henry Johnson, Eli Hays, General and Martha Myers, Aunt Sarah Denniston, the Logan Todds, Ann Ford, Thornt Clampitt and the Everett Eastons."

There were more, for the routes were long, and there was a family on just about every hill and back in almost every hollow. They included the Deckards, Martins, Sowders, Blackwells, Hilderbrands, Stancombs, Eads, Kinsers, Coveys, Bartletts and the Honeycutts.

"To have lived the life I've lived," Mack said at one point of our visit, "and to have known all those fine people, I guess I'm the luckiest guy living. In the winter they'd be waiting for me with hot coffee or tea, and sometimes even a sandwich. And in the hot months they'd have something cold for me to drink. They were all real nice.

"They'd want to hear what news I could bring them, too, because the newspaper wasn't available," he said. "And they'd ask about so-and-so down the road. I often took news from one home to another. They enjoyed my coming. They seemed happy. And I enjoyed seeing them. I got a lot of pleasure from the service I was extending to them."

Huckstering wasn't the easiest of jobs, and Mack's routes were not only long but also time consuming. They sometimes required that he be out until well after dark. Those were pre-television days in the country and house windows were darkened early. Henderson Creek, Dutch Ridge, Hunter Creek, Peerless, Goat Run and Chapel Hill and similar places could be pretty spooky after nightfall.

One night when Mack was weaving the big yellow bus amid the haunts and ghosts that romped on the gravel roads that ran in and out of those places, a tree branch reached out and bent a side mirror backward and through the window on the driver's side of the bus. That was the closest call he'd had with spooks on the routes, he said.

As he spoke it was as though I was listening to my own experiences as a huckster, for when Mack left that job I had become his replacement. I was an unemployed World War II Navy veteran when I first met Mack, and was sorely in need of work. It was he who taught me the huckster routes which I, too, would ride to a better future.

I had also become acquainted with a number of the customers of whom he spoke. In many respects it was a fun job. And sometimes it was spooky, too. One winter night as I was running late through Dutch Ridge I was momentarily blinded by a sudden, huge flash of blue and gold light. And just that quickly I was in the dark. The bus had shut down; no lights, no power. I couldn't imagine what had happened.

Alone in the darkness of that rural country, miles from home, and certain that a ghost would get me, I nevertheless began investigating my situation. It was not long before I discovered that the battery was missing. It had come loose from its supporting bracket and had fallen out of the bus. I suppose the big blinding flash occurred when the connections were torn loose, or when it hit the ground and exploded. What had been a battery lay in pieces, scattered on the gravel road. In spite of that I also enjoyed my time as a huckster, brief though it was.

As happened with Mack, I too met many fine people. There were a few who were not so fine. I could not have been aware of it at the time, but there were two, a husband and wife who, through the words of a relative, would re-enter my life a half century later. They were an elderly couple, when I knew them, and the husband was confined to his bed, the victim of a stroke.

While he was teaching me the routes Mack and I one day were ushered into the man's bedroom by his wife who wanted us to see her husband lying flat on his back in bed. He'd had a stroke, and he was unable to speak. I later would make a few sales at the house; one thing the woman never failed to buy was Booster Chewing Tobacco. It came in twist form and was packed in a cardboard container. Black and juicy, you could feel the moisture in it when you picked up a twist. She always bought two twists and would stick them down in her apron pocket.

It didn't occur to me that she was buying the twists for herself; not until one day when she again invited me inside for another look at her husband lying in bed. It was near lunch time and there was fried pork shoulder in

101

a skillet on the wood cook stove from which emanated the most tempting of aromas. When she offered me a sandwich I was unable to refuse.

While I wolfed the sandwich down at one end of the table she sat in a chair at the other end close to the stove and talked. It was during her discourse that I discovered the recipient of the Booster chewing, for every so often she would lean to one side and spit the blackest tobacco juice I'd ever seen or hope to see into a nearby coal bucket.

I was still somewhat newly arrived in Indiana from my New England home and although I had heard of pipe-smoking and tobacco-chewing Hoosier women, she was the first tobacco-chewing woman I'd seen. That I should witness it as I was eating became for me a lesson in self-control, for I wanted to throw up each time she spit. But the taste of fried pork shoulder between two grease-sopped slices of bread helped me get past that desire.

After leaving the grocery on wheels in my hands, Mack re-enlisted in the peacetime Air Force, obtained a college education, retired after twenty years, and became a school administrator. When we met the day I was driving through Heltonville he was enjoying retirement there with his wife Velma.

Unknown to Mack or me when we ran those routes was the existence of buried treasure at one of those rural homes. I learned of it several years after my visit with Mack in his front yard. Ever since I had huckstered there the history and early people of those rural areas had been a fascination for me. When I learned that Bloomington resident Seabert Sipes had spent his boyhood years on Dutch Ridge I was anxious to speak with him.

Mr. Sipes and his charming wife, Stella, were wed September 15, 1928, in the home of her parents, which stood where the Mental Health Center is on Rogers

Street, east across from Bloomington Hospital. They were planning their sixty-fifth wedding anniversary celebration for the following Sunday when I called; he was eighty-nine, his lovely wife, eighty-one.

Four years old when his father died, his mother, left with five children and working in a boarding house in East Oolitic for fifty cents a day, was forced to disband her family. She placed him with her sister and her husband who lived in a small two story log house on Dutch Ridge. Three of his siblings also were placed in separate homes. The mother kept a two year old girl with her.

The loss of his family, Mr. Sipes recalled, was very painful. Unloved in his new home, life was not easy for him. Young as he was, he was given work to do. There was so much sometimes that he would break down under its demands, and he was whipped severely for his innocent shortcomings.

"My uncle would lay out long rows of corn and potatoes and expect me to keep them hoed. Why, it was an impossible task for a kid, and he'd just about beat me to death because I couldn't get it done," he said.

"And his wife, my mother's sister, was a hell-cat. She was a Christian woman, though. I'd seen her go to church and clap her hands and jump around. But then she'd go home and say to her husband, 'You rotten sonuvabitch, you've been running with another woman.'

"I used to hide my uncle's whiskey," he remembered with a smile. "He made it down over the hill and kept a gallon of it behind the kitchen door. That's what he drank, and he had it for company, too. Of course he sold it to anyone with the money to buy it. He made whiskey all the time I was there. It was good whiskey. I had to help make it."

Mr. Sipes recalled that at age twelve he was forced to carry U.S. mail on horseback in rural southeastern Monroe County.

"My uncle had the route," he said. "In the winter time he'd come and take me out of school to carry it for him. I guess at twelve years old I must have been the youngest mail carrier in the United States."

He reminisced that the route began at the Heltonville post office and continued along Dutch Ridge to Allens Creek, where he visited Lewis Conner, the postmaster. He then rode back past the old cemetery there and up Wade Eads Hill. His horse then clip-clopped along to Hardin Ridge and around to the post office at Chapel Hill, where George Cracraft was postmaster.

Conner and Cracraft, both aware of the abuse he suffered, chose to say nothing about it. Child abuse in one form or another was common then, and it was considered family business. But in their own way the two men at least sympathized with the young mail carrier.

At long last the mail route ended in Smithville, after which, Mr. Sipes said, he would still have a long ride before getting home. Horseback wasn't the warmest way to travel, and he often suffered from the cold.

"My feet froze a couple of times," he continued. "I went home and sat behind the stove with a pan of cold snow water to thaw the frost out of them. That was the way to do it," he hurried to add when he saw my look of cynicism. "It's like when you burn yourself, you hold the burn over something hot to draw the heat out. That's the only way to thaw frozen feet."

He carried the mail route three winters. By that time his mother had remarried and was living with her new husband and family in Sanders.

"I'd think all the time why my mother couldn't have found out what was happening and got me out of there," he mused. "I remember one day when I was carrying the mail some people at Smithville dared me to go see her where she lived at Sanders.

"I did. I rode over there and told her I was unhappy.

104

After I told her a few things that had happened to me she advised me to leave my aunt and uncle. So I ran away," he said. "I was fifteen, and I went to work at the Showers Plant – on Rogers Street where RCA later built – for twenty-five cents an hour."

Reported as a runaway it was not long before he found himself in the custody of Sheriff Bill Bartlett. After listening to what had been happening to him on Dutch Ridge, and that he had not seen his mother or his siblings during that time, the sheriff was both angry and sympathetic. He declined to return him to his relatives. Instead, he allowed the boy to go back to his job. That was the beginning of the happiest time of his life.

"I'd had a hard life before then," Mr. Sipes said with a half smile. "But I've been happy ever since then. And that's really what matters. Oh, I hated for a while. But I got over it. I've had a happy life with my wife, and our wonderful children."

He named his children for me: "Wilma, Dolores, Patty, and Roger. And," he continued, "grandchildren and great-grandchildren, and great-great-grandchildren. I couldn't be happier."

Mr. Sipes said that his hatred for his aunt and uncle actually lasted until they got old and sick. Then he returned to Dutch Ridge to visit them, and he and his wife helped take care of the sick couple.

"I don't know, I just felt sorry for them," he said of returning to the people who had given him so much pain and misery. "My uncle had a stroke and he lay for a long time."

Stroke! Stroke? Mr. Sipes and I compared notes and I found it to be an almost incredible coincidence that Mr. Sipes' uncle should have been the same stroke victim I had seen lying in bed so many years earlier when I was driving a huckster wagon on Dutch Ridge. And doubly so that his wife, Mr. Sipes' aunt, should have been the same

105

woman who, more than a half century before I had called at Mr. Sipes' house, had fixed me that delicious fried pork shoulder sandwich and spit black tobacco juice into a coal bucket while she watched me eat it.

"When he died," Mr. Sipes resumed his account, "my aunt took me out on the place and I helped her dig up a gallon jar with a metal lid. It was filled with money. Maybe eight-nine thousand dollars."

The money must have been the accumulation of profits gained from years of selling whiskey that was made down over the hill from the two story log house. If the value of a pig in those early years had been equal to four plugs of chewing tobacco, eight or nine thousand dollars surely was a virtual treasure.

"We took the jar to a Bloomington funeral home and asked how much the funeral would cost," Mr. Sipes said. "It came to six-seven hundred dollars. I don't remember exactly. But she opened the jar and paid for it right there in cash."

The aunt is believed to have reburied the money on her land on Dutch Ridge. Later, when she became severely ill and had reached the point of death, she summoned a neighbor and asked him to notify her nephew to come to her bedside, that she needed to speak with him.

"We left Bloomington for Dutch Ridge right away," Mr. Sipes said of embarking on a drive of some twenty miles. "But when we got there she was dead. I'm sure she wanted to tell me where she buried that jar full of money."

Mr Sipes' aunt was interred in Todd Cemetery on Tower Road. I was there. At the time I knew nothing of Mr. Sipes and his experience on Dutch Ridge. I had always remembered the fried pork shoulder she had fixed for me and in spite of her chewing tobacco and spitting while I ate it, for some strange reason I wanted to be at her funeral. I had arrived late and I stood alone, watching the grave diggers fill in her grave.

In later years, long before I ran into Mack installing the old bell in his front yard at Heltonville, and long before I met Mr. Sipes, I wrote a newspaper column about that woman. Because I did not want to embarrass her even in death regarding her chewing tobacco, I referred to her as "Meg."

We had talked of numerous things while I ate the tasty fried pork shoulder sandwich that day in her house. One was church. Although Mr. Sipes in later years said she was a church-going person when he lived in the house as a boy, I don't think she was that day. She told me she had no use for nor need of church and preachers, and she added, "They's things that are right and they's things that ain't, and any damnfool oughter be able to tell the difference."

It was an unusual quote and it not only became a temptation for me to use it in my column, it also caught the eye and imagination of a Bloomington newspaper reader and woodworker hobbyist named Dick Frothingham. He tediously cut out each of the letters in wood and glued them to a backboard. He then cut out more letters in wood to read, "The full Gospel according to an old woman named Meg, as told by Larry Incollingo," and glued them under the quote.

The completed plaque was found and purchased at a gift shop by my editor, Bill Schrader, and his wife, Barbara, and it wound up above the door of my office at the newspaper where for many years it greeted visitors.

I sometimes had to explain to the over-curious that I had felt obligated to use the name "Meg" to save the woman embarrassment. Besides revealing her tobacco chewing habit, I had also noted in my column about her that while shoveling dirt onto her casket one of the grave diggers had spit brown tobacco juice into her grave.

Had their positions been reversed she might have done the same thing, who knows. And even though spitting

107

tobacco juice in her grave might have been appropriate, I didn't think it was very nice at the time. But who knows what I might have felt had I known how she and her husband had treated their little nephew. But, then, there was always in my mind the memory of that delicious fried pork shoulder sandwich.

While this replay of the past was on fast-forward in my head, Mr. Sipes had been quietly thoughtful. Then I heard him say, "I used a probe around there for a while, but I couldn't find it."

He was referring to the balance of the money his aunt and uncle had hoarded, the virtual treasure still buried on Dutch Ridge.

"It's a gallon jar with a metal lid," he explained. "Inside is a First National Bank leather money bag."

He looked at me and nodded his head, "I'm safe in saying there's eight-nine thousands dollars in it. When I helped my aunt dig it up there was a big stone across the top of it, so a metal detector was useless in trying to find it."

THE HOLDUP

There were five women in the branch bank at Gosport the day it was robbed by a young bandit armed with a double-barrel shotgun. One of them was Piney Brewer, a maiden lady of eighty-eight years, who had fifty dollars in cash stuffed in the cuff of the sleeve of her old-fashioned dress.

Another was Pauline Smith, a seventy-one year old former teacher and farm wife who held in plain view in her hand a wallet containing seventy-four dollars.

If you are scratching your memory, forget it, this happened a long time ago; in my time as a reporter, but a long time ago. I had forgotten it until I was reminded by Tammy Hamm of Owensburg. She was recounting how she and friend Josie Hayes were nearly involved in a bank holdup one day and Josie's unique reaction to the near miss. I'll repeat Tammy's account of that event after I relate the Gosport incident.

Piney had very nearly missed the holdup there. She had her hand on the doorknob to leave when the robber pulled it from her grasp and ordered her back into the building.

"He had a gun that long," Piney later told me as she stretched her arms as far as they would go. "He told me 'Get back in there.'"

She described the robber as an "overgrown teenager, a country jake," she said. "I was not in the least frightened," she said. "It seemed so much like a picture show, or something."

After a pause she added, "You know, he didn't look like a dangerous man. I don't believe he'd of shot anybody."

That is not what Josie Hayes thought when she and Tammy had their close call. But, like I said, I'll get to that after I finish this.

Piney had graduated from school in 1906 and joined the family business, a mill and grain elevator, in Gosport. At the time of the bank holdup she'd been there seventy years, all of her adult life. We spoke at her home after the holdup. Although she kept a locked screen door between us I was able to see that she was wearing a toboggan-like hat, a long coat and spectacles. She informed me she got caught in the bank when she went there to deposit some checks. She described how the robber had given the branch manager, Bernice Dittemore, one of the five women, a brown paper bag to fill with money. And how, before leaving the bank, he made the women get down on the floor.

"Then he left," Piney said. And she added, "I'll tell you the bravest little guy was Rosalie Weaver. She dashed out right behind him and got the license number of his car. I wouldn't have done that on fifty bets. She's a dandy person. And Pauline – Pauline Smith."

When the robber ordered the women to get down on the floor Piney had lamented aloud that if she got down she'd never be able to get up.

"I told her I'd be sure and help her up," Pauline later told me. "I had stood within two or three feet of him and I didn't see him until he said, 'This is a stickup. This is a holdup. This is . . . ,' whatever he said. I don't even know what he said. But I looked at him and thought, this can't be for real. He's going to say, 'Fooled you, didn't I?' or something."

She described the holdup man's weapon as, "An old shoddy-looking double-barrel shotgun he kept swinging around."

Like Piney, Pauline said she wasn't scared. Of course, Piney wasn't there to hear her say that. Piney said Pauline *was* scared. And, of course, Piney wasn't around to hear Pauline say that Piney was scared.

Both women agreed that the bank robber must have been scared since he missed the wallet Pauline had in her hand, and the wad of cash Piney had stuffed in her cuff.

Tammy and Josie's bank robbery experience came several years later at a branch bank at the "Y," on the Bloomfield Road. Because Josie didn't drive, when Tammy went to the bank she invited Josie to go along to take care of her business there.

Josie, who was born and bred in the country gained in her lifetime a modicum of fame for her home remedies. For that reason she is featured in my book "G'bye My Honey," the first edition of my Reunion Trilogy. But not in connection with this story. Tammy told this story after "G'bye My Honey" was published.

Like Piney, Josie, at the time of the Bloomfield Road bank robbery, was also up in years. And it was her custom after she conducted her business at the bank to get off her feet, to take a chair by some windows while she waited for Tammy to finish her business. The windows looked out on a sharp incline.

One day when the two women arrived at the

bank police cars with their red lights flashing and armed police all around gave the place an aura of unfolding intense drama. From bystanders the two women learned that a man armed with a long gun had just robbed the bank and fled. Although he had threatened people with the frightening weapon, no one was hurt.

It was a bit much for Josie. And thinking about how narrowly she and Tammy had missed being in the bank at the time of the holdup, she was left completely shaken.

"I'm sure glad I wasn't in there," Tammy said Josie suddenly blurted. And she said Josie went on to tell her listeners there at the bank that, "If I'd been sitting in there and he pointed that gun at me I would have jumped out the window, rolled down that hill, and sheeehut my pants!"

MINERAL

A motorist wondering at his whereabouts after driving into the tiny Greene County community of Mineral one day came upon Doug Roach by the roadside.

"Where does this road go?" he called.

Doug, a black-haired, black-bearded, six-footer who appeared twice his size in insulated, brown coveralls, replied with a twinkle in his dark eyes, "Chicago . . . California . . . where do you want to go?"

Fortunately the stranger was hoping merely to make it to Bloomfield, only a few miles away. He also could have driven to Chicago or to California from there, but it might have been tricky, because not just anybody can get to anyplace from Mineral. Say "Mineral" to the unwary and it can be as confusing as saying "Plummer," or "Park," or "Furnace," all of which are also rural communities in Greene County.

But Mineral is not quite as remote as all of this would imply. It used to be, and only a few years ago, too. But if one can get to anyplace from Mineral today, one can also get, with some care, from anyplace to Mineral today.

Oral Feutz (pronounced fights) and John Flake used to operate a store there. "Feutz and Flake," the sign across the front read. They ran the place together until Feutz sold out to Flake. A year or so later Flake sold it back to Feutz. And until Oral built a new store the name sign remained the same.

Amy Feutz, Oral's wife, used to display her oil paintings in the old place. Lois Harris, who also painted, was the hired hand and ran the old store while Oral was out buying up supplies. There was a warmth and charm about that ancient two story building; the store on the first floor, the Odd Fellows meeting place on the second. There was very little left of that structure at this writing: only the two brick columns that stood on either end of the gasoline pump island and supported the front end of the second floor.

Decades have passed since Oral and John went into business there. In that time Oral reared a family, built the new store, was baptized, had by-pass

114

Left to right beginning at bottom left:
Doug Roach, Bobby Burch, Herbie King, Terry Feutz

surgery and lived a quiet but interesting life in between, and later died. His son, Terry, was storekeeper for a time. The last time I looked the place was closed.

The usual visitors' bench was a part of the store's furnishings. It was immediately in front of the counter. A talking place, it was. And mornings usually found a visitor seated there, sometimes Doug Roach, Herbie King, Darin King, Bobby Burch or someone else. Bobby was a student at Indiana University and hoped to teach at Bloomfield High School some day. Sometimes Clifford Williams visited the store. Noontimes often found Olaf Feutz there; "Uncle Olaf," Terry called him. Oral's brother. He often was joined on the bench by Ervin Ramsey, and together they got into some "old time chats." Once in a while Jack Duncan visited while Uncle Olaf was there. Uncle Olaf stayed until closing time, when Terry would take him home.

In its own quiet way Mineral was a pretty exciting place, especially the store, which eventually had become "Feutz's," sans the Flake. Some called it "Oral's," or "The Mineral Store," or simply "The Store." It didn't matter. No one seemed to care what it was called, really, just so it was there, as John Coats would have said. John stopped at the store on Saturdays. A deck of cards, a card table and some folding chairs provided him and some others the means with which to play euchre, and they had at it, game after game until closing time. John told Terry once that his Saturdays at the store were the only relaxing times he had from life's fast pace. And to show his appreciation John made several purchases there every week.

"I don't want this little general store to get away," he once told Terry.

The card table and folding chairs were always available, not just on Saturday, and a visitor might have found a euchre game in progress almost any time, or be challenged to one. Even I. And one day I found myself paired with Bobby Burch in a game against Doug Roach and Herbie King. The latter were hurt badly, having suffered two losses out of two games when the contest was called because Terry was ready to close the store for the day. Driving away from the Mineral store that day I easily concluded that John Coats was right about what a stop at the Mineral store could do for a fellow.

Mineral was indeed a quiet place; so quiet it elicited on divers occasions strange answers to questions asked of its residents. For example, in response one day to Terry's greeting, "What do you know?" Doug replied, "I know two things. I know that a dog that weighs a ton is a heavy dog, and I know that I don't know nothing."

But for a tornadic wind that blew the roof off Oral's garage and laid it over on his pickup truck, and then blew a big barn off its foundation and knocked down some trees, little else had happened in tiny Mineral, expect for the chicken snake. Gilbert Haywood found it lying belly up in the Furnace school yard one Sunday and to scare Terry carried it into the store on the end of a stick.

It didn't work. Not with a chicken snake, anyway. But Terry did decide to try to awaken the thing. He put the snake into one of those large glass jars you sometimes see containing a long coil of pickled baloney, and displayed in some stores atop the meat case. Pickled baloney and a handful of crackers had more than once served as lunch for me on my rounds of rural Indiana for my newspaper. Quite often it was the only fast food available. It used to be pretty tasty stuff. But as time went by it seemed to evolve into a rubbery synthetic that left me with a ferocious heartburn.

These were the thoughts that came to mind when I saw some thirty inches of chicken snake occupying that jar. Only what was in the big glass jar this time didn't look like a coil of pickled baloney. Neither was it pickled. It looked exactly like a snake. A coiled snake; a sight which didn't necessarily give me heartburn but one which gave me tender feet, for I began tippy-toeing around inside the store, carefully watching where I stepped.

Thankfully there were no other snakes in Feutz's store. Just Doug Roach, Gene McGlothlin, Herbie King and Terry, playing the card game of Rook, and studying their hands and venting their little disappointments through Christian-like ejaculations such as, "Mercy! Mercy!" and, "That's what I say!" and, "Anyone who'd deal a hand like this ought to be shot!"

It seemed pretty certain to me that they had switched to Rook because on my previous visit I had

117

beaten them good at euchre. However, Terry insisted they just needed a change. Interviewing four Rook players who are concentrating on the game is not the simplest challenge I've ever undertaken. But I did learn that Terry had punched some holes in the jar's lid so that the chicken snake might have some oxygen; and it still wasn't showing much life. They offered some musing speculation as to why the snake was lying belly up in the Furnace school yard and why it was not in hibernation like all snakes should have been in winter.

"All we can figure," Terry said taking long pulls on his curved-stem pipe before pushing the smoking briar into his shirt pocket under his insulated vest, "is that somebody probably split him out of a stick of wood. Or the warm weather brought him out."

"I believe he came out of the ground," said Doug as he laid out on the tabletop a green card and added, "That's trump." He had one hand full of green cards and the other partially covered by a cast on his forearm. He said he'd been helping a neighbor move some cows and one of the beasts knocked him down.

I kept waiting for Terry's shirt pocket under his vest to go up in flames. Patient as I was the thing did not. I can't say that I was disappointed, but I did try to envision the kind of conflagration and interruption that would have brought to the Rook game.

Funny thing about snakes. Once I start thinking about them I can't get them off my mind. They just keep raising their heads, very much like my shaving cream gushing out of its pressurized can to coil unto my fingertips. I got to thinking that if the snake in the pickled baloney jar revived, and the nearer we got to winter's end the more likely it would, it probably would be released just in time to rear its head at some unsuspecting mushroom hunter. That was

118

The Old Mineral Store
Courtesy Lois Harris

Photo By Phil Whitlow

what they were looking forward to in Mineral at this time – mushroom season!

"The biggest one I ever found wouldn't fit in a skillet," Terry remembered a mushroom. "It had to be quartered to be fried."

When the Rook game was over it was time to close shop for the day. Terry took the pickled baloney jar to the rear of the store and stood it on its bottom, the chicken snake coiled up inside. He then checked that the lid was screwed on tight. Then he placed a heavy object on top of it without covering the air holes. Didn't matter. When I went out to my car I still checked the floorboards and under the front seat.

After I had written about my first visit to Mineral I learned that the world is almost completely made up of people who were born there, and that most of those who weren't are related to them. All seemed proud of their heritage. Yet, if you blink at the wrong time on the drive from Bloomfield to Koleen you might miss Mineral, it's that small.

I sometimes think about the Mineral store. Inside there was everything imaginable. And Oral. I recall one visit when I sat on the long bench and watched him sharpen a chainsaw on the counter across from me. As he carefully angled the slender file across the teeth of the chain he spoke of Mineral, Furnace and Plummer Creek, and what they were like in earlier times. It was during that visit, too, that in roaming about the large store and viewing the huge and varied inventory, I saw tins of White Cloverine Salve. The sight brought back some memories which I included in a subsequent column, noting, too, that I had seen the salve at the Mineral store.

"I sold a heck of a bunch of Cloverine Salve after that column came out," Oral told me afterwards. "It was the best advertisement I ever had, and it was free."

Kenneth Arlen Harris – 1942 or 1943
Courtest Lois Harris

That column also brought me a gift of a tin of the salve from Annabell Buskirk, of Bloomington, a tin I kept on my desk at the newspaper office to treat minor cuts, bruises, and the epizooty. It was never used, and I still have it someplace.

A visitor could turn up almost anything in Feutz's. During one of my last walks through its aisles I stopped before an array of Aladdin lamps. While Oral had his head turned I rubbed first one and then another – all of them – and no serving jinn appeared to do my bidding. Not even a jinni. I didn't say anything to Oral about that and I was later glad that I hadn't; I remembered that I didn't have the magic ring which is so important to the overall system of jinn. Until then I was inclined to believe that Oral's Aladdin lamps were phony.

The route from Bloomfield through Mineral to Koleen and beyond is a rural one and a traveler in

Mineral Store
Courtesty Amy Feutz

need of a convenience can't be too picky, as he would be, say, in a town full of filling stations. One day I did find what I thought might have been the original country convenience, appropriately named "Big John," painted in black paint on the white surface of the side facing the road. But because of its historical nature I felt that it would have been tantamount to desecration to have availed myself of it. Besides that there is something about those early American thunderboxes that I cannot abide, and I'm not one to go around with my nose tilted.

I didn't even peek inside. The weeds and bushes and vines were so thick I couldn't get around behind it. Moreover, half the people in Greene County picked that moment to drive from Mineral to Koleen and from Koleen to Mineral and slow down to look at me as they passed. And if Koleen Post Master Phyllis Allen wondered why I was shifting from one foot to the other while I was talking to her in the post office after I got to Koleen she now knows.

Phyllis was a Silverville girl – she was Phyllis Super before she married Max Allen of Koleen, a construction contractor. Her sister, Betty Glassco, still lived in the tiny western Lawrence County community. Phyllis mentioned that Iva Wagner was her Sunday School teacher there. Iva's husband, Walter, operated the store in Silverville for many years. Leatha Baker lived next to the store, and Onis Gore had the blacksmith shop – all so long ago. Phyllis was a relief clerk in Koleen for several years, and was appointed postmaster there February 26, 1978.

Back to outhouses, the little boy's and little girl's at the old Mineral School were separated by a coal bin. But they were gone, as was the school, which for years stood abandoned, a revered memorial of another time. Emptiness and loneliness had taken their place.

Once each year, on the second Sunday in September, the loneliness traditionally erupted in laughter and happy recollection as the little boys and little girls of long ago returned in shrinking numbers for a reunion in flesh and spirit. They came from all over Hoosierland, and from other states, complete with covered dish, and fading memories yearning for renewal. The Methodist Church across the road opened its doors to them and they gathered there for worship, and chatted in the new wing of the building. Like the old days when they were in school, they used, before the church was modernized, the men's and ladies' outhouses, which still stood behind the modern church building like white-painted errors in the chronology of time.

The day passed too swiftly. A day filled with programs, speeches, the revival of memories, and the awarding of prizes to the oldest living student, the youngest, and the one who traveled farthest to attend the reunion. Teachers were remembered – W.H. Wolfe, Nellie Jane Blackmore, O.M. Buckner, Earl Hudson, Mabel Stone, Fred Corbin – and their names rolled off tongues in a joyous-sad litany of the living and the dead, and the happy days once shared in a country school.

More than a hundred years had passed since the school was built. There were two rooms, one room held the first four grades and the other consisted of fifth, sixth, seventh and eighth grades. A coal heater took up the center of each room and on winter days those pupils seated nearest the stoves would move back after they got sufficiently warm, and the kids in the back rows took the seats closer to the stoves.

"It used to tickle the kids to death when a teacher told them to go out and get a bucket of coal," recalled Lois Harris, a Mineral School graduate. "There was no well at the school and we carried water more than a tenth of a mile from a neighbor's house in a bucket. You'd be surprised how fast the kids would get their lessons done just to be able to go get a bucket of water," she said, laughing at the memory.

Each pupil had his own tin cup which hung from a nail along one wall. A pupil's name either was stenciled on his cup or on the wall under the nail from which it hung.

"Every so often the teachers would make us wash them," said Mrs. Harris. She laughed suddenly and added, " The women teachers did. But the men teachers weren't so particular."

Classroom propriety back then wasn't quite as stringent as it might have been. She recalled one male teacher who chewed tobacco and spit in the same corner during the entire school year.

"It splattered all over the woodwork, and at

Christmas time we'd have to wash it clean for our Christmas program," she said through gritted teeth and a wry smile.

Kids walked from miles around to attend classes. Some had to cross Plummer Creek, just south of Mineral, which runs into the West Fork of White River. Others walked along the Monon Railroad tracks and they passed the Monon depot. Sometimes on the way to school they saw and waved at the crew of passing "Old Nellie" – their name for the Monon train.

"The tracks and depot are gone now, since forty years ago or more," Mrs. Harris said, "but you can still follow the old rail bed to Avoca, Oolitic and Bedford, or Switz City in the other direction."

She believed the winters were colder back then, and people dressed for them too.

"Our underclothing was made of outing flannel, and we wore long underwear and black stockings. I had a good serge dress and my mother had made me an apron for each day of the week and I wore one over my good dress at school. The boys wore long underwear, too, and overalls with galluses," she said.

The long cold walks ended with the coming of horse-drawn school buses.

"Ours was an enclosed wagon pulled by a team," she continued. "There was a heating stove under the floor and the stovepipe chimney ran up the side of the wagon. The fire was fed from the outside. We could see the smoke from the chimney long before we saw the bus coming. I rode one of them for seven years."

The community was known as Mineral City back then, a bustling village and surrounding farm folk. It devolved to a spot on a road in south-central Greene County, a spot whose romance with life was remembered by a precious few, and whose name had

125

fallen victim to the hatchet of time. Mineral. That's what those who didn't know and never shared in its glory called it. Mineral, a once bustling place laid waste by progress and consolidation.

But even on a wintry day in the middle of the week the sun still rose there as brightly as it ever did, maybe brighter. And those who did not move away, those who stayed in or near Mineral, remained generally warm and friendly. It has been said there that those who left through the years took some of that warmth with them to kindle the hearths of a cooling world, that a little bit of Mineral has been scattered abroad. Lucky world!

During his final illness, Pete Ledgerwood asked his painter sister, Mrs. Harris, to do an oil of Mineral City, and to include in it "Old Nellie" as it approached Haywood Crossing. A newcomer to Greene County might better understand were he to know that the Monon Railroad ran through Mineral from 1875-1934, and that Dick Haywood once lived near a grade crossing on the Mineral-Koleen Road.

Mrs. Harris did the oil; a view from The Backbone, a hilltop on which she was born and still lived. From that distance she was able to include in the painting the Old Bee Hive, an area that included the David C. Roach home, the Russell Huffman house, the Ralph Chipman place, Bill Veatch's Plummer Creek, Mt. Zion Cemetery and, of course, Old Nellie approaching Haywood Crossing.

When she delivered the painting to her brother it was to learn that it still was not quite complete – at least not to his satisfaction.

"Smoke," Pete told her. "When Old Nellie was approaching the crossing the engineer would blow the whistle and you could see smoke (actually steam) puff up from the locomotive."

Returning the work to her home, Mrs. Harris painted-in the smoke that Pete had asked for. He was pleased. Before the year ended he passed away. The painting was returned to Mrs. Harris.

Mrs. Harris' interest in art went back to when she was a child, when the Ledgerwoods couldn't afford oils and she "doodled" with pencils and crayons. She and her husband, Clarence, reared their family in a house on The Backbone. Her mother called the hill "Kooler's Knob." Because he said it was always cool up there, Clarence called it "Windy Ridge."

Mineral School was erected as a one-room institution in 1860. In later years another room was added and it continued as a two-room schoolhouse until it was abandoned in 1951. Sometime during its midlife, a pretty young woman named Gertrude Wantland took up teaching duties there. Although she enjoyed the small school she yearned to have a school bell that would call her charges to classes.

"To get the money to buy one she promoted a pie supper," Mrs. Harris spoke from notes she had kept through the years. "And a bell was bought with the proceeds."

She could not provide a date. Later, however, that kind lady dashed over some two and one-half miles of country road to Smith Cemetery to obtain the date of the teacher's death.

"Gertrude taught only a few years," Mrs. Harris said. "She contracted an illness and died very young."

The marker on the grave at Smith Cemetery bore that out: Gertrude Wantland was twenty-two when she passed away in 1913. When the school was abandoned the Ladies Aid of the United Methodist Church bought the building and thus acquired the bell. When the aging structure was later razed, the bell was stored at Henry Hasler's home.

When the Ladies Aid was granted enough space on church property for that purpose the bell was enshrined in a six-by-six brick enclosure, a piece of Mineral history dedicated to posterity.

After asking in and around Mineral it soon became evident that memory was hard-pressed to recollect crime there. There had been few if any problems there. No gangs. No rights demonstrations. No social tensions. Nothing. Except for an occasional euchre or Rook game. Mineral had been notoriously peaceful, an uneventful place. Uneventful, that is, except for the nighttime break-in at the church October 29, 1994.

"They must be getting pretty desperate when they break into and destroy things in God's house," church member Martha Ellen Williams said of thieves who made off with more than fifteen hundred dollars of church property.

She said she didn't expect anyone to take "God's house" literally, "But," she added hopefully, "it might make whoever broke in feel ashamed of themselves if they read that in the paper."

Stolen were two large speakers, six microphones, a sound system control box, brass candlesticks from the communion table, and two wooden offering plates that had been part of the church for as long as Martha Ellen could remember.

"Maybe," adduced Jim Letsinger, who was baptized in the church in 1928 and whose two hundred eighty-seven acre farm joined the church property, "he (the thief) plans to be a traveling evangelist and figured he would need the collection plates. They have no other value. They're just old wooden plates."

The church, a large, clean white structure at the west edge of Mineral, combined a sanctuary, a community room, and Sunday School classrooms. Thieves (Martha Ellen said she was possessed of a visceral feeling there were three) broke a rear door window to gain entry to the building. In addition to the thefts, they pulled Christmas decorations from a closet and scattered them. Then, as might be expected of vandals, they took down a fire extinguisher and sprayed its contents around until it was empty.

The break-in was discovered by Gilbert Hayward who was driving past the next morning. Gilbert thought the door had been left open by Clarence and Lois Harris, custodians of the sanctuary and the classrooms, or by Martha Ellen, who cared for the community room. But a few telephone calls quickly put that thought to rest. A few more phone calls and everybody in and around Mineral also knew of the break-in, and they were appalled that anyone would dare do such a thing.

After their feelings were made public in a subsequent column that I wrote about the break-in some of the more important items taken were mysteriously returned, for which Mineralites were grateful.

Although it was said there was no crime before that in Mineral City, there was an *incident* that occurred during the community's heyday. As native Jim Letsinger remembered the story, a stranger appeared in the saloon there one freezing winter night. He could have arrived on foot, or he might have jumped off a passing train. Anyway, he was glad to be inside where it was warm. However, at closing time he was turned out into the cold. Hoping to find a warm haven for the night, he knocked on the door of a residence and implored the man who answered to give him shelter for the night.

It so happened that the gentleman who lived there was a school teacher and part-time preacher, Letsinger recounted. Under different circumstances he might have yielded to the stranger's plea and let him in, but because of the late hour, and especially because he was a stranger, the householder feared for the safety of his family and turned the man down.

It is not known if he knocked on other doors that night, for no one else came forward to say. But this much is known. The luckless stranger ultimately made his way to the railroad depot and tried to find some comfort from the bitter cold in the lea of that building. He was found there the next morning, frozen to death.

There was little need for ceremony. The stranger's frozen body was taken by wagon about a mile north of town to where the church used to be before it was moved down into Mineral. There it was laid to rest in the small burial ground that bears the name Mt. Zion Cemetery.

From that story Jim, at my request, recounted a personal experience from World War II that left me wondering if he would have lived to return to Mineral had not the huge ramp on his LCT malfunctioned as it raced for the beach at Normandy on the morning of June 6, 1944.

When the big bow door was lowered it disappeared into the sea. As the boat plunged forward, ocean water rushed through the massive opening. Try as they might the crew could not raise the ramp; it apparently had broken off. They backed off then and again tried for the beach. More sea water rushed in.

"We were knee-deep in water in the boat," Jim stretched his memory as he reviewed that unforgettable morning.

The LCT had begun its dash for the beach with two M-7s bristling with artillery, two trucks, fifteen men from the 58th Armored Artillery, and a dozen or more medics with the 500th Medical Collecting Company aboard, all sorely needed on the beach. With the crippled ship in danger of sinking they could do nothing but sit and wait for orders, for help. They would come, but in the meantime the war was passing them by.

Jim was astride a farm tractor disking a section of his land along the blacktop that runs through

Mineral when I interrupted him. A slim, wiry man who wore the chin strap of his farmer straw hat fastened against the dusty wind that swept his field of labor, he halted the big machine and climbed down. After we shook hands he led the way across the road to a cool room in the church annex.

"I joined this church in 1928," he remembered as we took chairs at a table. "The minister was Paul Haywood. He lined up all four of us kids, my two older sisters and our little sister, and me. He sprinkled us and we got our membership certificates right then and there. You don't hear that much today."

Because the blacktop separates Taylor and Richland townships kids who lived on the north side of the road went to high school at Bloomfield and those who lived on the south side went to Scotland. The two groups wouldn't see each other all week until Sunday School at the church.

Jim was born and grew up on the north side of the blacktop, where he lived with his wife, Elizabeth. They had no children. He farmed close to three hundred acres and some of it, where he was disking when I interrupted his work, was on the south side of the roadway. He had told me on a previous visit that the solitude of farming often gave him time to think about how his ancestors struggled to hold the land that was then his.

When I asked him about farming he replied that it was a lot of work. "Especially when it's about twenty degrees below zero and you've got to go out and feed the stock," he said. Then to make a little joke about the weight of his burden he smiled wryly and added about Elizabeth, "I've just got an old woman for a helper."

They were not married when he went overseas. His ship put in at Liverpool and for a time he was stationed at Torquay, a summer resort in

Devonshire. Movies, a civic orchestra, a theater and a soccer field, made his stay there a pleasant time. But behind the scenes preparation for a big military show was taking place. The curtain went up before daybreak June 6, 1944.

"We couldn't get to the beach because the ramp was broken off our ship," Jim continued recounting his experience of that day. "We were never in such a situation, and we didn't know what to do. We wore inflatable life belts, but we were medics and carried so much stuff on our backs, plasma and so on, we were afraid if we got in the water we'd just roll over and drown. So we waited. About six o'clock that evening an LCP picked us up and we got to the beach about six-thirty."

By that time there was only a scattering of sniper and mortar fire, but Jim and his medics, one of them John Ellett, from Bloomfield, were unprepared for what they saw.

"It was a horrible sight. Enough men to equal the population of Bloomfield were lying out there dead," he remembered. "We were told to dig in till we got our bearings. Then we put the wounded on stretchers and carried them to aid stations."

If Jim was unprepared for viewing the many dead of the historic invasion, he was less prepared for an encounter with a dying GI, an encounter that left a never to be forgotten memory with him.

"After we started picking up the wounded," he began relating that meeting, "I tried to give a fellow plasma. He was semiconscious. He reached up and took hold of my arm and gripped it very tightly, and he mumbled something. I presumed if he was saying anything" – Jim's face began to redden – "it might have been –" Jim hesitated, unable to go on.

Then he said, "Of course when you're dying I presume you think of the person you love the most, and most of us at that time were not married, so probably he was thinking of his mother, and probably –," Jim hesitated again, overcome with emotion. Then he said, "Maybe he was trying to say something like, 'Tell my mom I'm sorry I won't be coming home . . .' "

Jim was suddenly choked up. His eyes welled and glistened and he tried to smile and clear his throat and speak at the same time. If I understood him correctly then, he said, "That makes me cry just to think about it right now . . ."

Mineral is four miles from the Bloomfield public square. On some Saturday nights during his high school years Jim walked the several miles from Mineral to Bloomfield to attend the picture show there. The first show was at seven o'clock, but there were times when he didn't arrive in town until eight and he'd stay for the second show.

"The second show let out at eleven o'clock and I knew I'd have to walk home," he remembered. "And I'll tell you that was a scary walk for a high school kid. There were no lights in houses. Everyone had gone to bed. And that road past the highway garage was always scary. There was a swamp in there and it was always foggy and the frogs would go *ker-chounk, ker-chounk, ker-chounk.* I really made time along there because that was really scary. And there was always a dog that would come out barking at you. Normally I could walk the distance in an hour, but on Saturday night after the picture show I could do that distance in half the time because I'd run half the way."

PRAYER POWER

Jack and Esther (Ett) Withem didn't get carried away with their first wedding anniversary as some folks do.

"We celebrated only moderately," Ett told me. "We had a piece of cake, and that was about it."

It was not a piece of just any cake, though. When they were married a year earlier Ett had put the top layer of their wedding cake in the Withem freezer, and they shared a piece of that. Maybe that's a common practice, but I'd never heard of it and it sounded sweet enough to me to want to tell you about it.

"We don't get in a great big crowd too often," Ett said of celebrations. "We're not like that. Besides, our anniversary fell on a Sunday and that's usually a pretty full day, anyway, by the time we go to church and come home. Maybe," she said hopefully, "we'll take a little trip this fall."

A little fall trip is what Ett and Jack settled for instead of a honeymoon after their June marriage. A grass farmer, Jack was quite busy and he told Ett, "I'll take you to Texas in the fall, when the harvest is over." And he did.

Ett was one of those people who liked to go all she could. Jack, on the other hand, had to make hay while the sun shone. And when their anniversary was just a few weeks away she told herself, "I'm afraid he'll be too busy farming to take me anyplace."

But that wasn't important. What was important was that Ett was happy. Happier than she'd been in a long time.

"It's been just wonderful being married to Jack the past year," she confided. "We're just more in love all the time."

Jack, who'd been silent all this time spoke up and said, "Our love just grows."

Before Jack came into her life Ett was pretty lonely. Her first husband Paris Withem, a distant cousin to Jack, had passed away in 1977.

"I was awfully lonesome," Ett remembered. "Then one night I prayed to get over it. I said, 'Lord, please send me a sweetheart. A decent one.' And Jack knocked on my door that very night."

Ett, a religious lady, believed Jack was heaven-sent. And though it was a coincidence of loneliness that brought Jack to her door (his wife Nina died in 1978), and Ett knew Jack was lonely since he told her he was, she said she would never change her mind. Jack, she insisted, came to her in answer to her prayer.

"He just wanted to go to church with me," Ett recalled. "It was Easter Eve, and he was so lonesome, and the Lord sent him to my door."

Fourteen months later they were married. Ett was sixty-three; Jack was sixty-one. Ett brought nine children to the marriage, Jack three. Between them they also had several grandchildren – say about thirty-seven? And when Rev. Leonard K. Eddleman tied the knot a good many of their children and grandchildren stood by as witnesses.

"It was short notice," Ett said of their decision to get married and the early date they had set. "But," she said with a satisfied smile, "most of them were there."

The short notice was by design. Ett and Jack simply did not want a big to-do over getting married. Still, when their children learned of Ett and Jack's plans, they came up with some plans of their own.

"We waited until the last minute to tell them," said Ett. "They got so enthused they wanted to throw a really big one, but there just wasn't time. At that, though, they got a pretty cake, and they put all the usual trimmings on our car."

Ett revealed this account of their wedding one morning in the Green Door, a clothing bank at the rear of the Civic Center, in Spencer. She was employed there as a member of the Green Thumb Project. It was on a subsequent visit to the Green Door that I was to meet Jack, a well-built man whose appearance belied his years.

Ett was about five feet tall and had bright eyes that seemed to blend with the colors she wore both times I'd seen her. When during our first meeting she spoke of her loneliness and said, "Then one night I prayed . . . ," I felt impelled to write this. Although it has never happened to me, every so often I hear a similar story – "I prayed and my prayer was answered," someone will tell me.

Of course I wonder about the validity of statements of that kind. But they seem always to have some kind of proof, much as Ett had offered proof. I remembered one lady telling me, "The Lord never fails me. He sends me whatever I ask for."

When I call for a hand like that I routinely get a zip. But, then, I must ignore or sleep through important knocks on my door. Ett, on the other hand, did respond to an important knock. She was not asleep when her prayer was answered. And she was very happy for having prayed. I believe her happiness was genuine and the result of prayer because she said so. I also believe, and I'm glad that I do, that true love need not be restricted only to the young.

"It makes no difference that we are older," Ett said.

"It's just as wonderful as a young couple's marriage. If you're older, like us, you're just more sure of what you're doing. But no matter what your age, it's just wonderful to be in love."

She had one hope for the future – no more – and that, in her own words, she expressed in this manner: "I just want to be a good wife to Jack," she said.

Millions do what Ett did. Surprisingly, many, like her, are rewarded for their effort. Take the case of a holy hundred dollar bill that showed up at the office of a chiropractor one day. Not my name for it – his, I was told. Maybe it was holy – is. Who knows? You be the judge. In any event, I was told he planned to frame it. It's a long story, but you'll find it worth your time.

It begins with a patient needing some X-rays in the amount of ninety dollars. A forthright, sincere lady named Theo Stillions had been having back problems. She lived on Handy Road in a neat white house with new siding. Her two daughters and their husbands had it put on to keep her from painting it. They thought painting the house would be too strenuous for an eighty year old.

Theo didn't think so. She'd painted her house once before. She also did some painting at Blackwell Church. A relative pastored there and he'd been renovating the place and she lent a hand, painting around the windows.

Blackwell was a long way from Theo's home, but not so far that she wouldn't drive it. She drove all over the place, including to her own church, The Church of Jesus Christ, on Miller Drive. A very active person, she made candy that she took there, she made cakes for the YMCA, too, and she baked bread for friends and neighbors. She also quilted, babysat, and sewed to earn extra income.

During a visit in her kitchen she told me that the

night before she was born her pregnant mother was sitting on a nail keg watching her father working in the garden and her father said, "Tomorrow is Good Friday. If it doesn't rain I'll plant potatoes."

At four o'clock next morning it starting raining. When Theo was born two hours later her father, who had hoped for a boy, suffered his second disappointment of the day. But, the doctor only charged him six dollars for delivering her, Theo said.

"I was cheap," she told me, "but I lasted a long time."

She graduated in 1932 from the old Bloomington High School that stood on land that later became Seminary Square, and she started cooking in the school cafeteria kitchen that same year. She cooked there ten years, and more than twenty years at Sanders School. Because she had little choice in the matter she was also the first cook at Bradford Woods, Monroe County schools' summer camp for kids.

"We can't have the camp unless you go up there and cook for us," Superintendent Frank Templeton told her one day in 1956.

Theo spent three weeks there and spent her weekends preparing foods to be served at the school the days she was gone. She quit cooking in 1974 to care for her husband, Aubrey, who was ill. When he died they had been married fifty-two years.

"He was the greatest man who ever lived," she told me. "And he was a wonderful father."

Because she was unceremoniously dropped from the group insurance plan she'd carried for many years, Theo invested what she could in another policy. But inflation had been taking regular bites out of its benefits. Because she lived on a Social Security stipend she could not afford the money to buy more insurance.

"If I don't hurry up and die," she said wistfully, "there won't be enough left of it to bury me."

It was because of high costs that ninety dollars had the sound of big money at the chiropractor's. Theo didn't have it. Where was it going to come from? The chiropractor offered her a generous payment plan, but Theo was uncomfortable owing anyone. She didn't know what to do.

There are many people, like Ett and Theo, who, when their lives reach a point between a rock and hard spot, turn to an old friend. And that's what Theo told me she did. On the drive home from the chiropractor's, she said, she had a talk with God.

"I talk to God just like I'm talking to you," she told me. "And I told Him I had to have these X-rays and that I was worried because I didn't know where the money was going to come from."

It was a fairly good ride from the chiropractor's to Handy Ridge so it wasn't a short talk. But Theo said God was an old friend and she was used to such long talks with him. She was baptized seventy-five years before I met her, she'd been a steady church-goer all her life, a loyal tither, too, and she'd talked to God every day, she said. She didn't give up easily, either. One of her longest talks with Him lasted thirty-eight years and ended only after her husband gave up and allowed himself to be immersed in a baptistery, she said.

Theo felt she didn't have thirty-eight years to wait for ninety dollars, so she must have put on the pressure. When she got home she hadn't been there but a few minutes when there was a knock on the door. A stranger was there with some intricate sewing for her to do. When the woman asked how much she would charge, Theo, who said she had always stretched her Christianity to the limit, replied, "Oh, whatever you want to pay me."

The visitor reached into a pocket and brought out a hundred dollar bill. "Will this be enough?" she asked.

Theo was totally unprepared for such a quick response from her friend. Here was not only the ninety dollars she needed for X-rays, but an extra ten dollars to tithe. She burst into tears of gratitude. She had to explain her behavior to the startled visitor, and she later told the whole story at the chiropractor's office.

After she finished talking Theo said the chiropractor told his receptionist, "Don't do anything with that hundred dollar bill. I'm going to frame it. That's holy money."

There are a million stories out there like Ett's and Theo's. Over the years I have listened to many of them, and I've wished numerous times that such good things would happen to me. But, to repeat myself, when I call for a hand like that there's an "Out To Lunch" sign on the door of Ett's and Theo's old friend.

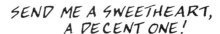

SEND ME A SWEETHEART,
A DECENT ONE!

JOHN B. JONES

Over the years seasonal high waters had washed away a piling under the old Hunter Creek school house at Yellowstone and that corner tilted down toward the creek. Still, classes there continued six months a year in spite of that. They took up between eight and eight-thirty in the morning and continued through four in the afternoon with one hour for lunch.

"On the last day of school it was customary for school patrons to spread a big dinner at the school for the teacher," recalled John B. Jones, a former teacher there.

Jones when I spoke with him lived in a comfortable, handsome dwelling with his wife, Zula, at 235 Church Lane, Clear Creek. He was in his eighties. A teacher in Monroe County for twenty-five years, he taught at Hunter Creek during the school year of 1909-1910. During the summer he was a peddler, or, as he put it, "a huckster," who drove a horse-drawn wagon laden with all manner of merchandise and food that he sold or traded to farm and hill folk in Monroe County and bordering Lawrence County.

The Hunter Creek class of 1909-1910 consisted of Ray Fleetwood, Ophie Mitchell, Floyd McPike, Leston Murphy, Oma Mitchell, Ivan Murphy, Luther Wray, Basil Mitchell, Leston Jones, Ocie and Oka Mitchell, Carrie Elkins, Macie Mitchell, Goldie Murphy, Glenn

141

Jones, Esta Murphy and Effie Fleetwood. There were also Lenza Wray, Glenn McPike, Anna Elkins, Harry Lutes, Berlie Fleetwood, Verna Wray, Ray Fleetwood and Sylvia Wray.

The mother of the Mitchell girls fulfilled an unexplained personal desire by giving each of her daughters a first name beginning with the letter "O", Jones recalled. Teachers also did some giving – on the last day of school – in those days. A souvenir folder bearing a photo of himself on its front, a list of the names of the members of his eight classes on the inside and a nostalgic poem about the last day of school, was presented by Jones to his pupils.

"Some months ago we gathered here
To work together day by day;
But now the time to part draws near,
And we lay all our books away."

That is the first stanza of the poem received by that class of 1909-1910 – first grade through eighth grade.

"I began teaching at eighteen," Jones remembered. "And Hunter Creek School in Yellowstone was my first school."

It was from Yellowstone, from the store of his brother, J.W. (Jerry) Jones, that two horses, Ted (named after Theodore Roosevelt), and Winfield (namesake of a famous judge of that time), heaved and snorted into the harness and pulled the huckster wagon with Jones in it to the surrounding country homes.

"I had a horn that was about five-feet long," he laughed, "and I'd blow that thing when a farmhouse came in sight."

From Yellowstone he traveled on Mondays toward Heltonville on the Bartlettsville Road which then ran somewhere near Knob Creek. The roadbed was hard with muttonheads (geodes). His route took him into

142

rural Hunter Creek then wound around to Bartlettsville where he ate "dinner" with the Curtis Sowders. After that meal he spent the afternoon selling and trading his way to Chapel Hill and Allens Creek. His Monday nights on the road were spent at the home of Mr. and Mrs. Dan Chambers.

"Dan fed the team, bedded them, I was fed my supper and given a bed to sleep in and the next morning they gave me breakfast, all for only one dollar," Jones recalled. "Then before I left they'd trade that dollar out at the wagon, and buy more."

The wagon bed was ten feet long and about four feet wide. Its sides were extended perhaps another foot in width by built-in racks of shelves on either side, and its rear extended well beyond ten feet because of a high rack of built-in shelves there.

The entire high back was enclosed by a single large tailboard and, when Jones was selling and trading, this was dropped to form a counter which was propped up by a heavy board. The large opening exposed bolts of cloth and other materials tucked into the neatly constructed compact shelves. Then the entire wagon — or traveling variety shop — was enclosed with a weatherproof black material.

"On my second day I'd go out Fairfax Road and eat dinner at Charlie Wisley's, then I'd back-track across the Nancy Jane covered bridge and on to Sciscoe's Branch," he traced the old route from memory.

That second night he took supper and a bed with Mr. and Mrs. John P. Sciscoe. His third day found him moving eastward to Burgoon Ridge, then south to Dutch Ridge and down the Polly Helton Hill, over to Hunter Creek again, and then to Yellowstone and home.

"I'd take butter in trade and it wasn't fit for eating because there was no way to keep it cold. I used to toss it into a barrel on the wagon and it would become oil. We shipped that butter oil to the soap factory," he said.

Butter was ten cents a pound; eggs eleven or twelve cents a dozen, and old roosters were traded out at two or three cents a pound. Shipments to and from his brother's store were received or sent from Heltonville on the Milwaukee Railroad; except salt, which was drayed to a store at Norman Station.

Jones was born in 1889 in Brown County. The nearest post office was at Elkinsville, three miles away. As a boy he worked the after end of a single-furrow chill plow behind a team made up of a horse named Ned and a mule called Andy. He roughed it with an old spike "A" harrow and tended corn with a double shovel.

He was one of three children of Elizabeth (Lizzie) Bates Todd, a school teacher. When she later divorced and moved her family to Burgoon Ridge, in Monroe County, to teach at the Burgoon School, Lizzie met and married a farmer by the name of Alexander Jones, a widower with eight children. During the course of their marriage Alexander and Lizzie had seven more children.

"An old neighborhood Dutch woman always regarded the last seven children as being 'Of the third litter,'" Jones laughed.

Alexander's holdings were such that when he died in later years each of the children received about ten acres of ground. Because he died intestate, however, his material possessions were sold at auction.

"Four ewes and four lambs brought twelve dollars; one stand of bees, a dollar; one trundle bedstead, twenty cents; one scythe and cradle, twenty cents; one red cow, thirteen dollars and fifty-cents," a list of goods sold, and treasured by Jones, reads.

Terms at that auction were cash for any purchase of

five dollars or less, and over that amount purchasers were given up to nine months to pay. The sale 'grossed' two hundred and sixty-seven dollars and eighteen cents.

"I had only an eighth grade education," Jones said, "but my mother insisted I become a school teacher. I took a few months training at Central Normal and got my teaching certificate."

Long before his career was to end he was to receive from the state superintendent of public schools a certificate authorizing him to teach all subjects in all grades one through junior high school.

"That's not bad for an eighth grade education, is it?" he joked.

Jones was small in stature, five-feet-three, and weighed about a hundred thirty pounds. Although the wavy mass of black hair that was his when he began teaching school at Yellowstone, and when he reined Ted and Winfield around the countryside of Monroe and Lawrence counties, was gone, he still had more hair than many men half his age. His eyes were as revealing as the written word, and blue and laughing.

When we met he had come a long way from the farm in Brown County, and old Hunter Creek School in Yellowstone. Along the way he taught at Axson Branch, Tanyard, Burgoon Ridge, and Robertson schools, all of which were gone at this time, and ended his teaching years at Harrodsburg.

Also along the way of those years he escaped the flu epidemic of 1918 when, "People died like flies," of diphtheria, measles and other killer diseases, of that time. Probably because Lizzie regularly fed her family a mixture of sulfur and sorghum molasses, and quinine, Jones said. He escaped, too, an occasional outbreak of head lice almost common to school rooms in those early years.

As was the life of the pioneer school, his was a full one. And in his retiring years he had much to remember. In the little souvenir folder he gave to his 1909-1910 class at Yellowstone an ode to "The Pioneer School" summed up the nostalgia of those memories:
"Yonder it stands, as it did of youre (sic.),
Its work is done, its reunions o'er,
The blocks alone mark the chimney place,
For the mortar no longer fills the space.
All are gone, never to return again."

THE HUNTING HORN

Stories like this one are passed around and I'm pleased to pass this one on to you.

A farm widow telephoned a veterinarian and complained that her donkey was ailing. The animal had been her late husband's pet and was advanced in years and probably should have been put down, but she was determined to keep it alive for as long as possible. She referred to the animal by name, which she pronounced "Jerry-miah." Could the doctor come out.

"I'm eating dinner right now," the vet replied. "I've also had a pretty long day. Why don't you just give him a big dose of mineral oil. If he's not better by morning I'll drop by and take a look at him."

"But, but –" the good woman stammered. "How do I give a donkey mineral oil?"

"From a big bottle," the vet said.

The woman gasped. "Won't he bite me?"

"Come now," the vet spoke kindly. "You're a farm woman. You know about these things. If you're afraid he'll bite you give it to him the other way, through a funnel. You know."

She'd seen sick cows and horses treated that way on occasion, but by her late husband, not by her. Out of dire necessity she had treated her children that way when they were small, yes. But they were children. The thought of treating an animal the size of Jerry-miah that way, well, it made her nervous.

147

Nevertheless, hoping in her charity to bring the sick animal some relief, she eventually forced herself to go to the barn. The ailing Jerry-miah, his head drooping almost to the floor, stood heaving massive groans and moans.

"Poor thing," she said to herself. "I've just got to try to help him."

At a small workbench along one wall she searched for a funnel she knew should be there. In her nervous state she couldn't find it. During her search, however, she spied her Uncle Zeke's hunting horn hanging from a nail. It was a handsome, polished instrument, with long, colorful tassels hanging from it.

"Why not?" she mused.

She quickly took the horn down, then reached up to a shelf where she believed the medicines for treating animals were kept. With increasing nervousness she groped anxiously and grabbed what she thought was a bottle of mineral oil.

She grasped the hunting horn and hurriedly did what she was supposed to do with it. Testing it to see that it was securely in place, she then poured a liberal dose of the liquid into its wide mouth.

When it reached Jerry-miah, the animal suddenly straightened up to almost twice his normal size, legs stiffer than four fence posts. He released the loudest bray ever heard in the surrounding farm community, then the aged donkey reared up and plunged through the barn wall. C-R-A-S-H! Splintering it.

The farm widow was astonished. Could mineral oil have such a sudden rejuvenating effect on an animal as she had just witnessed? Maybe she ought to give herself a shot of the stuff. Then she looked at the label on the bottle. "TURPENTINE," she read. "Omigod!" she exclaimed.

In the meantime Jerry-miah cleared the barnlot in a single leap. The five-foot fence that enclosed it might

148

just as well been a line drawn on the ground, he cleared it so easily. Then he sped down the road at a double gallop, a gait rarely seen in donkeys. Every fourth time Jerry-miah's hooves hit the ground, the hunting horn would release a blast of sound.

That horn had been heard before. Uncle Zeke had blown it many times on his numerous fox hunts. And fox hounds in the farm community were familiar with that sound. They knew when they heard it that Uncle Zeke was going hunting. So here they came arunning from every direction, north, south, east and west, and took off down the highway, apanting and asnarling at the hapless Jerry-miah's heels.

It was a sight to challenge the talent of the most gifted artist – Jerry-miah going at top speed, doing that double gallop. Uncle Zeke's polished hunting horn in that most unusual position. The long, colorful tassels aflying out behind. The sweet clarion notes issuing forth at equally spaced intervals. The hounds arunning at Jerry-miah's heels, their red tongues hanging out a foot. And their yelping and yawping harmonizing with the sweet sounds of the hunt coming from Uncle Zeke's hunting horn.

Over the rolling hills of southern Indiana they ran. Down through the hollows they charged. They passed the log home of Ol' Clyde Farrow who'd been drunk for as long as anyone could remember. Ol' Clyde saw the passing procession and stared in disbelief, his mouth hanging wide open. He swore he was having a day-time nightmare. He joined Alcoholics Anonymous that very day and has been a devoted member ever since.

Jerry-miah and his entourage, meanwhile, had plunged noisily onward into southern Indiana toward the Ohio River. Hearing the intermittent blasts coming from the hunting horn, a dozing bridge tender, thinking it was a string of barges approaching, dashed to crank up the bridge. In his mad race from the burning pursuit, Jerry-miah did not see the opening in the bridge floor. He plunged through it to the river far below, where, much to his relief, the cool water gurgled and glub-glubbed into Uncle Zeke's hunting horn. Splashing and yawping in the water around him were the many hounds that had been hot on his heels.

As the story goes, the bridge tender, at the time, was a candidate for county sheriff. On election day he polled only three votes--his, his wife's, and his mother's. The rest of the voters in the county figured that a person who didn't know the difference between a jackass blowing on a huntng horn and a river boat wasn't fit to hold public office.

ELZORA AND VIRGIL

The old Buick was about as full as it could be as it bounced from Bono toward Bedford. Squeezed inside were Elzora Pate; her father, Everett, who was driving the car; her mother, Della; Elzora's sweetheart, Virgil Holt; and his mother, Lucinda.

Elzora and Virgil were on their way to the Lawrence County Courthouse to obtain a marriage license, and to be married.

The old folks were making the trip to be witnesses at the knot-tying ceremony. They needn't have bothered; there would have been witnesses enough without them.

Unknown to them as they drove toward Bedford, George Harris, the preacher they'd expected to perform the marriage ceremony, was at that very moment on the second floor of the courthouse serving on a jury.

After they arrived at the courthouse the judge presiding over the trial was informed by the bailiff that the anxious couple awaited without. When he was also informed that when told the preacher was "tied up" Virgil had moaned, "But we can't wait," the good jurist recessed the trial long enough to give the preacher time to do his primary duty.

"There we were," said Elzora at the couple's mobile home on R.3, Mitchell, one day. "All of us; me and my mother and father; Virgil and his mother; the preacher; the judge; and the whole jury, standing out there in the hall outside the courtroom while we got married."

Under a headline that read "Couple Couldn't Wait," the unusual ceremony that took place in an equally unusual setting made the next day's paper. Fifty-eight years later,

151

when I visited with Elzora and Virgil, that same wedding was about to make the newspaper again.

Elzora had been courted six months before Virgil proposed. One of eight children of an itinerant portable sawmill operator, she was born in Ft. Ritner but lived in Bono at the time. She returned there with Virgil after each of them had said "I do" and promised for better or for worse.

"Virgil was so shook up he forgot to put the ring on my finger until we got back in the car," Elzora laughed at the memory.

She worked the time-worn ring off the third finger of her left hand and held it out for my examination.

"It was engraved with flowers all around," she touched it lightly with the tip of a finger. "Now look at it, it's as slick as a ribbon."

They spent their first night of wedded bliss with her sister and her husband, Louise and Henry Brown, at their house on Sugar Creek. Then they moved to a tiny shack that measured only a dozen feet square on Virgil's father's place.

"We had just enough room for a stove to cook on, a table to eat on, and a straw-tick bed to sleep on," Elzora said.

They lived happily ever after in that little shack until the first big rain came – one night.

"The roof leaked," she remembered as she and Virgil laughed at the memory. "We moved the bed around as much as we could, trying to find a dry spot. Finally we gave up and took off across the field in the rain to his father's house."

They laughed some more.

"We didn't care," Virgil said. "We was in love then."

Elzora agreed and added, "And that wasn't the only leaky roof we ever lived under, either."

She was seventeen on her wedding day, April 18, 1931. Virgil was just four days shy of his twenty-first birthday. When we met she was seventy-five and Virgil had celebrated his seventy-ninth birthday.

They were the parents of seven children; one, a daughter, was killed in an auto accident in 1971 and left six children of her own. In addition to those six the Holts had another twenty-three grandchildren, forty-three great-grandchildren (and one on the way), and one great-great-grandchild (and expecting another).

The years they had spent together were good ones, they avowed, and because they were, Elzora and Virgil remembered them as having been generally short ones. But they were not necessarily all easy ones.

"We've had our ups and downs," Virgil observed. "But we don't both get mad at the same time."

Elzora smiled. "We are both hard of hearing," she said "Sometimes we get into arguments but we can't hear each other."

When he was courting her, Virgil used to run the railroad tracks from his house in Mitchell to Elzora's in Bono, and then back to his own, a distance of several miles. He had worked at manual labor all of his life. He was still hard as a rock and he proudly punched himself in the chest and belly to prove it.

"I never made much money," his blue eyes beamed under the turned up brim of his teal blue "76" cap. "But we did have a lot of fun."

A CHEERFUL GIVER

It was around seven o'clock on a weekday morning. As I descended the long flight of stone steps from St. Vincent de Paul Church in Bedford I saw a dirty, unshaven figure huddled on the lowest step by the painted black pipe banister upright. With little or no effort on my part I could have been repulsed by him. That is until I saw the crutches by his side. I wondered what he was doing there.

"I hate to bother you, Mister," he quavered as soon as I got within earshot. "But you see how I'm all crippled up with *arthuritis.*" He held up two gnarled hands. "And my legs hurt so bad. I'm weak, and I'm awful hungry. I wouldn't ask you, but I have to have something to eat. Would you give me some money to buy some food?"

Before I realized it an overwhelming pride took hold of me. How fortunate, I thought. Having just attended morning mass and received the sacrament of Holy Communion I was being blessed by the presence of a beggar in need of help. Somehow, through this derelict, I was being singled out for a great act of charity. Despite the irreverent audacity of it I puffed up with more pride. Of everyone in town – ME! I thought.

I dug a dollar out of my wallet and, because he couldn't seem to close his arthritic fingers over it, I stuffed it in his shirt pocket. For me that indeed was a great act of charity for I had hungry kids at home. As I handed him the money I said something to the effect that he should get himself a good breakfast. At that time a dollar would have bought me a good enough breakfast, I knew, so I thought it should have done as much for him.

The dollar got me an unsolicited sad life story. Briefly repeated, he had been married, lost his wife and his job – both after he had been stricken with "this crippling " affliction. He turned to drink and began doing some terrible things about which he thankfully did not elaborate. He later found the Lord, quit smoking, drinking, and began living the good life. He gave me the whole bit. Holy or not I was beginning to get bored, then I saw what I thought was the shine of tears in his red-shot eyes. That got to me.

"Why don't you go inside the church for a few minutes," I suggested with puffed-up piety yet with a great deal of sincere sympathy. "It might make you feel better."

"I wish I could, son (I was much younger then)," he moaned in reply. "I wish I could. But, you know, I hurt so bad, and I'm so weak because I haven't eaten in so long, I don't think I could climb those steps."

Touched deeply, and on the verge of tears, I urged him on his way to a restaurant, before he should collapse right there. After all, I told myself, why prolong his agony. Even a poor unfortunate person like myself can only stand so much misery and suffering in his fellow man.

"Go," I urged. "Go. Enjoy."

At the newspaper office a short time later I needed little excuse to blurt to my colleagues how I'd

155

been chosen early that morning to feed the hungry and minister to the suffering and the broken in spirit. After hearing my description of "the poor old thing," as I had described him, someone exploded, "He's one of the worst winos in town!"

I was stunned. As a reporter I had prided myself in knowing everything, everyone – especially the bums and boozers – in town. And I had allowed myself to be stung. In front of church, yet. My religious experience of earlier that morning went right down the proverbial drain and Satan himself took over. Out the door I went, BANG! Into my car I jumped, SLAM! Raced up town, VROOM! VROOM! And I caught up with *Arthur* – Weak and Hungry – *Itis*, shuffling along on his crutches. I began tailing him, watching for him to go into some tappy. I planned to follow him inside, grab the drink from him, pour it over his lying head, and whack him with one of his crutches. He didn't go into a tappy. It took him the longest time to shuffle a few blocks where he turned into the concrete walkway that led to a well known rooming house on North I Street. I nailed him.

"I thought you were hungry?" I fumed.

Surprised at my sudden appearance, he gestured with a crutch toward the two story rooming house with curtainless windows, "I am, but I'm going to eat in there, they're waiting for me," he whined.

Before I could say anything more, an old codger who'd been listening at an open second story window leaned out and laughed. "Heh-heh-heh!" he chortled. "Did he tell you he was hungry? Come up here son, I've got a bridge I'd like to talk to you about."

I shut him up and turned back to the guy on crutches. I pointed in the direction of a restaurant

156

named "Epie's" and said, "Why don't you go over there and eat?"

"There should be some food for me in there," he whined, and again he lifted a crutch toward the house. "They cook it every morning for us."

"Go in and find out," I almost shouted.

He struggled up the porch steps, an effort that brought from him what seemed to be excruciating pain. As I watched his struggle I began to feel like a clod. I again began feeling sorry for him.

Once he gained the porch, though, he slipped the crutches from under his arms, leaned them against a swing hanging there, and walked briskly to the rear of the house. I began seething again. In a few seconds he reappeared and shouted, "I can eat here."

In a flash I was up on the porch. "Give it back," I said confronting him with my hand extended.

He grabbed quickly at his shirt pocket where I had stuffed the dollar. He mumbled something unintelligible, and stood there pouting, unmoving. I snatched his hand away and retrieved my dollar. I took a step backward and shook my finger under his nose.

"If I ever see you panhandling in front of a church again I'm going to have you arrested," I promised him. "Understand?"

"You mean you'd turn me in," he whimpered.

"In the blink of an eye!"

Judging from the look he gave me then I got the feeling that his arthritic heart was broken. Driving away from there I wondered what Mr. *Arthur Itis* would do for wine when the shakes hit him. I wondered lots of things. Eventually I began turning on myself, wondering why I had allowed myself to get so unreasonable, so angry. I wondered what differ-

157

ence it would have made if the guy had spent my dollar on wine.

Suddenly I found myself consumed by conscience. Then I began hearing a little voice. "The Lord loveth a cheerful giver," it kept saying. Then the little voice admonished, "Go back to Mr. *Arthur Itis.* Apologize. Give him back the dollar."

But I could not bring myself to do it.

Instead, I detoured to St. Vincent's. There I climbed the stone steps and went inside (churches were left unlocked then). I walked directly to the poor box.

"There," I told my conscience as I slipped the folded dollar in the slot. "If you have any more to say about this matter you can take it up with the present owner of the thing."

And I went back to the newspaper office.

BEEHUNTER

It took twenty-six chickens to save the life of Ira Fearnot after he was bitten by a rattlesnake.

The life and death drama took place in a house that stood like an oasis in the green and brown quilted flatlands in Greene County. Beehunter, they called the place.

Bushrod was only a mile up the road. The same slag ridges on the distant horizon that encircled it also formed an undulating garland around the sprawling patchwork of bucolic splendor.

The railroad tracks that ran through Bushrod sliced the land, too, and intersected with another track to form a huge V. The house at Beehunter sat within its slanted brackets.

"My own mother split those chickens right down the middle and put them on uncle Ira Fearnot's snakebite until all the poison was drawed out," recalled Louis William (Bill) Jones over a cup of coffee brewed and served by his wife, Clarabell, in the comfortable kitchen of the house.

There were a million memories there in the kitchen, the entire house, out where the rails intersect, where Goose Pond used to be, and Bill and Clarabell had them all. They were Beehunter – they and their son, Larry.

"As far as I know," Bill said smiling, "I'm the only

man who ever owned a town. A feller asked me if
there was such a place as Beehunter and I told him
to look at a map and he'd find it in the same size letters as Ellettsville."

In letters only, and on a map, was Beehunter ever
as large as Ellettsville. At its beginning the population was four – and but for a railroad telegrapher
and the children of Mark and Mary Alice Fearnot
Jones, and Bill's and Clarabell's children, there
never was what you'd call a citizenry there.

Mark and Mary Alice arrived there about seventy
years prior to my visit. The old Indianapolis-
Vincennes Railroad, later the Penn-Central, was
completed, and after that came the old C. & St. L.,
later the Milwaukee, that connected Bedford to

Terre Haute. Together the two connected the product of coal mines behind the slag ridges on the horizon to the fires of homes and industries of that time.

In the wilderness that lay beyond Goose Pond bee trees were in abundance. Bee hunters came from surrounding cities to search out the hollow trees of honey bees and gleaned the hives of their treasures. The honey they bartered, or gave away, but the precious beeswax was sold to factories from whence it emerged in the form of candles and polishes.

The railroads, the coal mines, the swarms of bee hunters, combined to attract Mark and Mary Alice to that lovely place. And it was there that Bill's mother opened Alice's Grocery and Restaurant, and his father, who took employment with one of the railroads as a freight and baggage agent, also offered a livery service to bee hunters.

Alice's Grocery and Restaurant thrived. Mark did well in the livery service. Miners on their way to and from the distant coal fields caught and rode the trains through there. It was the end of the line for the bee hunters. And it was the jumping off point for drummers who arrived with as many as ten trunks of wares at a time, and took lodging in one of two rooms above the restaurant.

When the chugging steam locomotives sighed and hissed to stops in front of Alice's it was a signal for her son Joseph to board the coaches with trays of sandwiches for the tired and hungry passengers. And Bill's job was to furnish buttermilk to the engineers and firemen at ten cents a gallon.

"There was just me and Joe," Bill reminisced. "Our sister, Ola Geneva, died of whooping cough, pneumonia .and brain fever when she was 15 months old. Joe and me were kept busy when the trains came in. There was more money changed hands on these railroads than in Bloomfield. There was times old John Webster sold more than three hundred dollars worth of tickets just for one train."

Webster was one of the original population of four in Beehunter. The others were Mark, Alice, and Joe, Bill's brother. Webster roomed above the restaurant. Seven miles southeast of there the West Fork of White River flowed on its way to the Wabash. In 1913 it raged out of its banks to create the worst flood in its history.

"The railroad platform was stacked full of mail bags that was going south. They covered the whole platform. That's why they used to call this the end of the line. When the river overflowed into these flatlands you sometimes could get south and sometimes you couldn't," Bill recalled.

Mark Jones operated the first school bus in Washington Township. It was pulled by a team of two horses, one, Old Tom, was sired by the famous Dan Patch.

"He was a beauty," Bill said, "and he stood all of fourteen hands high."

Facing the V of the railroads from the kitchen table where we sat, the long room to the left was once Alice's Grocery and Restaurant. It had been converted to a guest room of sorts with double bed, baby crib, and a collection of antiques and some more of the million memories of that place.

The walls were painted tongue and groove ceiling boards nailed horizontally to studdings and gave them the optical illusion of supination. Had I been lying abed they might have given the impression of a whole room at rest. It was in that room – long years ago – that Harry Whaley paid Alice five dollars and thirty-two cents for twenty-eight meals served him between September 10 and 19, 1905.

In yet another transaction that year a patron of the grocery store settled his account on October 9 for groceries provided him almost daily, beginning on September 22. The total bill — ten dollars and six cents.

Alice kept a ledger of groceries bought and sold, each meal, all income, all expenditures. Each item was painstakingly entered day after day, year after year. Perhaps the most painful entries were those surrounding the sickness and death of her only daughter, Ola Geneva. February 16, 1908, Alice entered a two-dollar expenditure which was in payment of a doctor's house call to treat Ola Geneva. The little girl died February 24. Two days later, the ledger showed, five dollars was paid the minister. And a month to the day after the doctor's bill entry, there was this one: "May 16, 1908, paid John Davidson, undertaker, Lyons, twenty one dollars and twenty-five cents."

Ola Geneva was buried in the family plot at Walnut Grove Cemetery, a six hour trip by horse-drawn hearse. Alice, under the date of February 26, two days after the child's death, entered into her ledger, "Livery for funeral, ten dollars."

Mark and Alice Jones had long since joined Ola Geneva, and uncle Ira Fearnot, in Walnut Grove. They had left behind the romance of memories to slake the curiosity of a wanderer, and to fill the house for years and years to come. The walls of the warmly congenial rooms were covered with photographs dating back to those early days, and dozens of other mementos, and chairs, beds, pianos, furniture, all enhanced the impression.

In the evening when the Penn Central and the Milwaukee diesels approached the intersections of the two rail lines that formed the very bottom of the

V, the sound of their horns carried over the miles and miles of flatlands to the slag ridges on the horizon where mournful echoes were born and returned like ghosts of days, and people, and trains of another time.

But the population of Beehunter was real, alive, happy, and they wouldn't have lived any other place. For that was home to Bill and Clarabell. Home, where they were enjoying forty years of marriage, where they raised five sons and two daughters, where fourteen grandchildren and their parents came to visit, and Bill's brother, Joe, came too, all putting the ghosts to flight.

DUKE

You can't take anything away from Duke because he didn't graduate. Not every disciple of education who attended classes in the little river town of Tunnelton did. But according to native son and long-time resident Louie Ingle, who knew Duke better than anyone else, you couldn't have found a more cooperative and willing scholar.

"He would sit at a desk in class just as attentive as any kid there," Ingle remembered Duke with fondness. "He never made any trouble, and I'm sure he learned a lot. I don't know if he ever got a diploma. If he did I should have it, but I don't. I felt he should have got some kind of award."

Had there been an award bestowed on him the honor undoubtedly would have been duly framed and placed alongside a photograph of Duke in the Ingle home. The picture was prominently displayed on the wall over Ingle's favorite recliner from which he spoke with me during my visit with him one day.

"He liked to go to school," Ingle said.

"He was part of the family," said Ruth, Ingle's wife of fifty-eight years who was seated in a chair opposite mine.

"You had to watch him," Ingle continued. "In those days cars had running boards. If you didn't watch, when you got to town you'd find him lying on the opposite running board."

Ingle paused. Then he added somberly, "He's buried on the family farm, between Tunnelton and Pinhook."

Duke was expert at riding running boards as he was at

165

sniffing out quail, and he was better at that than any other pointer in southern Indiana. Although it was feared that the unusual and dangerous habit would shorten his life, it was not his love for riding running boards that in the end put the great hunter in his grave.

"He was the fence-jumpin'est dog I've ever seen," Ingle began to recount the tragic event of Duke's demise. But before going any further into that final episode of Duke's long life, let's go back to the beginning of this story. The bird dog was a gift from Ruel Steele's uncle Al Steele, in 1927, when Duke was about a year and a half old. That was a halcyon time in the small rural community. The Great Depression was still in its future. Theron Huddleston had a thriving store across from the school, L.P. "Punch" Hall operated a popular restaurant, and Cyrus Allen was proprietor of the town's hotel. There was a blacksmith shop and a sawmill there, too, and Ingle's father, Homer, owned the general store which included the post office, of which he was postmaster. Consolidation had yet to lay bare the town's classrooms, and neon lights had not yet beckoned its youth.

This was the antebellum Tunnelton into which Duke was given, and it remained his home for the next seventeen years. A friendly nuzzler, his acceptance was immediate and general. His best friends were the town's kids, and he let them ride him as they might a small pony around the school yard. When the daily mail arrived via the S&T Railroad, Homer would package the Ingle family mail at the post office, hand it to Duke, and the pointer would carry it across town to Cora, Homer's wife, at the Ingle home.

In spite of all the love showered on him, all the fun he was having, the hunting dog never once forgot the mission to which he was born. He was a hunter of game birds. And he pointed and flushed them in such abundance as to become the respected and beloved champion bird dog for many counties around.

"That dog hunted six days a week," Ingle said of the popular animal. "My brother and I, and everybody else in town, hunted him.

"Sometimes," Ingle's wife quietly interjected, "he was hunted seven days. But that seventh day was against the law."

"From the time I was twelve years old, until I was forty, I could find fifteen or sixteen coveys of birds a day," Ingle recalled. "I guess I've killed enough birds to fill this room," he gestured toward the small room around us. "A good many of them with Duke.

"You can't do that anymore," he observed. "Times have changed. If you find four or five coveys now in this part of the country you'd be doing good. I could, probably, if I had a dog that was any 'count."

Apparently Duke, in his time, was just about as account as they came. Ingle ought to know. He once raised bird dogs, and people came from miles around to buy and trade at his place. When Duke's notoriety was at its peak, bird hunters from far and wide brought so many breeding bitches to him that his blood, Ingle was confident, still pumped through the veins of the country's better bird dogs.

Ingle continued: "Duke was the greatest dog I ever knew. And, like I said, he was the fence-jumpin'est dog I ever knew, too. Never a fence stood in his way. I never saw anything like him."

The venerable Duke met his fate down around the churchhouse. While the pointer was doing what he did best a barbed wire fence suddenly loomed before him and, as he had always done before, he leaped without hesitation. Up, up he went, long and lean, smooth and beautiful in flight. It was a jump that would have gone down in the annals of local hunting-dog field events, but it would not have been recorded as Duke's best jump. Alas, not quite enough of the great pointer's underside cleared the top strand.

"Snagged on the sharp points of a barb," Ingle spoke the appalling words as reverently as he might have recounted his own body being torn asunder.

167

The horror of the accident still gripped Ingle. "I'll never forget it," he said with a shake of his head. "Duke was hurt so bad. We rushed him to the vet, but he couldn't do anything for him, it was hopeless. We had to put him to sleep."

Duke had been gone a long time when I visited the Ingles. The school he attended, the children he let ride him, the good hunting days, were also long gone. Except for Ingle and his wife, Ruth, who take the time to remember him, the great bird dog has been forgotten. Yet, when southern Indiana fowlers take to the field the champion hunter, although unseen, is there, coursing through the veins of the best of their pointers.

MARIE'S

It is a curious fact of human nature that associations with some of the people who come into our lives thrive on little or no knowledge about them. Given a minute, the names of at least a dozen could come to mind; in that pause you probably can come up with the names of a few yourself.

Marie Boyer is an example for me. She'd been operating a gasoline filling station in Freedom for fifteen years when I met her. An old church bench and a couple of aging chairs inside the small building were as welcoming to me as was Marie. And it naturally followed that her place should become a haven of rest; and gasoline for my car, a soda and candy bar for my bodily energy, and stories, as told by the natives who lounged there, for my pleasure. More than that, Marie's was a place to regroup the senses, a place to come back down to earth.

It was not unusual, then, that a stop there should lead to a newspaper column. And another. And another. Marie, an avid reader of our newspaper, seemed to include in that zeal subjects whom she thought should appear in my column. And on my arrival at her station she usually would say almost breathlessly, "You ought to go and see so-and-so. That would make you a good article."

She was never wrong – at least about the subjects.

It was also not unusual that Marie should nod or point to a lounger in the station and say. "There's an article for you." Sure enough there usually was, such as Maxine Kay. Maxine wasn't lounging, she was standing at the door, anxious to be gone after paying for gas, when Marie singled her out. "She'd be a good one," said Marie.

Maxine, I learned, was then in her twenty-fifth year as a school bus driver. Moreover, she'd driven that long without an accident. And she hoped to remain accident-free until her retirement which she planned four years from then. She was one bus driver who enjoyed her work.

"I don't make that much money," she said. "So you see, it has to be love. I love the kids."

She carried at least forty-six of them daily to and from school in a sixty-six passenger bus over a twenty-two mile route. At one time she and her husband, Owen County farmer Gene Kay, both drove buses. But after eight years Gene decided it was the farm for him. He and Maxine had two children, a daughter, Roberta Morgan, and a son, Richard, a teacher at Owen Valley High School.

In answer to a question about her love for kids, Maxine said, "Well, you meet some fantastic kids, and you meet some ornery ones. But they don't stay ornery for long on my bus. I straighten them out. Then they're loveable."

Another of Marie's "article" tips was one of calling my attention to the steeple on the United Methodist Church. "We have a new steeple," she said one day in that breathless way of hers. "Our minister's father came all the way up here from Alabama to put it up."

Preacher Edwin Jernigan's father did in fact travel from his home in Columbia, in southern Alabama, to build a steeple on his son's church.

170

"He said once, 'You have a nice church, but it does-n't have a steeple on it,'" Preacher Jernigan recalled his father's words that led to the erection of the spire. "And one day my sister called from Alabama and said, 'Dad's on his way up there to build a steeple on your church.'"

L.W. Jernigan was moving too fast, and his son had to rein him in. Certain rules had to be followed, certain details required attention. But when the way was cleared, and the hundred twenty members of the church came up with the "aye" vote and the money needed, up went the steeple. The elder Jernigan had help from the men in the congregation and in a week the thousand pound steeple was installed atop the twenty year old structure. Then the elder Mr. Jernigan painted it, every inch; and he was eighty-three years old. When he was finished he refused to take a single penny for his work. He brushed it off by saying simply, "It's my gift."

The steeple rose seventeen feet above the point of the roof of the church, but its height takes nothing away from the manner in which it arrived in Freedom. In Columbia that grand old man was a retired car-penter who just couldn't remain retired. People who knew him for years came to him with all manner of home maintenance problems, and he tried to help them. He even built a steeple on a rural church there. People around Freedom, and Marie especially, con-cluded that Preacher Jernigan was certainly fortunate to have an earthly father like that.

It was a series of those kinds of homey bits that came from my stops at Marie's, and introductions to such people as Junior Johnson, Ward Smith, and Clayton Miller; and hearing from Marie that folks in Freedom were pleased with Patty St. John, our news-paper motor route carrier who, with her infant son on

171

the seat beside her, delivered their evening and Sunday papers.

Marie seemed always concerned for my health, and for that of my loved ones. "You've fallen off," she'd say when it appeared to her that I might have lost weight. "Your color is good," she'd say another time. "Is your family well?" she'd ask. For many years we went on that way. And I? Funny, but I was never that curious about Marie, until now. Oh, but I loved her. One day I did ask a few questions, only a few, but their answers told me so much about my dear friend. Wherever she is now I'm sure she won't mind if I share some of them with you.

When I met her Marie had been pumping gas at that station ever since the death of her husband, Harold Bruce Boyer, who died at age forty-seven when she was forty-three.

"No," she let the word linger as she spoke while making a wry face in answer to my question about remarriage, "I didn't want to. I saw the problems others had, and I just didn't want any of it."

At the time of his death her husband had been selling gas in Freedom for nine years. An established business, it offered a livelihood, so Marie became the station operator, the attendant. She was not sorry for her decision to pump gas. "Life's been good to me," she said to me one day. "The people too."

Life was work – seven days a week from seven-thirty in the morning until eight-thirty at night. At that she called herself "lazy," and she scolded herself (with a smile) for sleeping in until almost opening time of a morning. She took breakfast at home, lunch across the state highway at A. Z. and Lenora West's store and restaurant, and she had someone come in for an hour at suppertime so that she could go home to eat and stoke and bank the fire in the wood stove. Nearing

172

seventy, she was performing the same tasks she had asked of herself at forty-three, only at a slower pace. But she hadn't stopped. She did not intend to.

"What would I do if I quit?" she asked of the both of us. "I'd be lost," she went on to answer herself. "I'd miss this station if I didn't have it. Hadn't I just as well stay here as someplace else?"

Late one night Marie was in the kitchen of her home, not too far from the station, watching "Dark Night of the Scarecrow," a television movie, when a robber broke in. She was beaten and, afraid for her life, she handed over her filling station money.

"It was like something you'd see on 'Gunsmoke' on the television," she said. "I'm not used to that sort of thing. I never had anyone push on me my whole life. I could hardly sleep that night for my heart beating so fast, and missing beats."

After that fitful night of heart palpitations Marie seriously considered leaving the station. But after state and county police assured her they would find her assailant, and a procession of sympathizers and well-wishers marched to her door, she took courage and decided to stay.

"I'm not afraid, now," she said when I called on her after hearing about the assault and robbery. "I trust our law. Right from the start they began working so hard on this. I know they'll get him." They did.

Marie also had something to say about the people of Freedom.

"There are a lot of good people around here," she declared. "A lot of them have come to see me. They said they were sorry, and wanted to know if they could do anything to help. One brought me some turnips, and one brought me a piece of cake. People are awful nice around here."

She had said as much to me once before, on a cold,

173

blustery winter day. Marie's was never a self-serve station and some of the men who traded with her would pump their own gas when it was cold and then go inside and pay her. She took their word for amount and cost.

"I've known most of these people most of my life," she said of doing business in the tiny Owen County town. "I don't believe anyone is going to cheat me."

There was a little funnin' going on in Marie's when I arrived there one morning...

"This Liar's Bench," Clay 'Shorty' Auten laughed at Rev. Earl Ramey, pastor of the Church of the Nazarene, as he indicated the old church bench along one wall of the station, "is an old pew that came out of your church."

Rev. Ramey was attired in something less than clerical cloth; a red cap with a long bill, a plaid shirt and overalls. He returned Shorty's laugh and got in his own lick: "No it didn't," he retorted. "It came from the Baptist church right down the road there," and he pointed out a window of the filling station.

Wherever it came from it was then in Marie's and when the "liars" got off it you could see that it was painted a pea-or light-green. On this particular day there were plenty liars coming and going. One of them looked out another window and said, "There goes old Ad, on his way to the river again."

Marie said Ad Knoy was about eighty-six years old and, she added, "He got sick last week and they had to take him to the doctor. He gave us all a fright."

"Now he's going fishing," said Shorty.

Sure enough Ad was going fishing, with two dogs following him as he crossed the state road toward the West Fork of White River.

They called Shorty Shorty because he appeared short while seated, and he did seem short while seated on the Liar's Bench. As a four-or five-year-old child, he once told me, he and some bigger kids were playing a game called horse and rider (a form of piggy-back fights, I guessed) and one of the bigger boys fell on Shorty and, "broke every rib in my chest, and broke my spine, too," he said.

That, he said, was why his chest protruded as far out as it did, and that his legs developed normally but his chest did not. He'd have been six-feet tall or taller if it had. He'd been orphaned long, long before that accident and was living with an aunt and an uncle and their seventeen children when it happened. He later went to live with a grandmother. Shorty spent a lot of time at Marie's after his retirement.

"He's a mighty good jack-of-all-trades," said Marie. "But we don't impose on him as much as we used to."

They didn't. Shorty was only fifty-four, but he had to retire because of a heart attack.

"That's right," said Shorty. "One day my heart just blowed up on me."

There were four chairs in addition to the seating capacity of the Liar's Bench at Marie's. Claude Strouse had plunked himself into one about the time John Stahl pulled up outside in a pickup with a Hereford bull in the cattle rack.

"Hereford," Claude snorted in disapproval. "The best bull is a mixture of Hereford, Angus and Shorthorn."

That's the kind of cattle Claude was running just north of Freedom. When I told John Stahl what Claude had said, John calmly replied, "Now that's a matter of opinion. But I'm not going to fall out with him over it."

"Is this for sure a registered bull?" I asked John after stepping outside with him. I still don't know why I asked it, I wouldn't have known a registered bull from a Sears Roebuck riding mower. Not then, not now.

"He sure is," John said.

"Does he have a name?" I asked.

175

"Yeah," said John. "He has a name. But I don't know what it is right now."

"What do you call him when you can't remember his name?"

"I don't," John said tacitly. "I generally just go after him when I want him."

Back inside the station there was a lot of talk going on. Clayton Miller – from Coal City – sat quietly, taking it all in but culling most of it. Earl Miller wasn't saying much, either.

A reporter from a big city paper had been through Freedom a few days earlier and had taken a picture of Postmaster Margaret Knoy raising the flag in front of the post office. When her picture came out in his paper it was over a caption that read: "Dying Town."

Freedomites didn't take too kindly to that, nor to that reporter, Freedom will never die, people said after that. There used to be about thirty-five hundred people there at one time. That was back when Ad Knoy had a timber business, and pulpwood was a big business, and they loaded two or three carloads of hogs or cattle out of Freedom each week. There was a tavern there, then, too, known as The Barrel House, and Light's Hotel had about twenty or more rooms for traveling salesmen, and the old Pennsylvania Railroad's big black steam locomotives huffed and hissed and hooted in and out of town.

Shorty was quick to say that the people of Freedom were not dying. And he added, "I went to the doctor this morning and he said I wasn't dead yet."

When I asked John Stahl how long a bull was good for, he answered: "F'r as long as you want to keep him." And after a couple of seconds of thought he added, "Just like a man, by golly."

And somebody from the Liar's Bench snorted, "Just like a town, by gosh!"

All this time Marie was making trips out to the

drive to pump gas. When she got a break she smiled at the talk and said, "I like it here. The ladies come, too, you know, and sit around and talk just like the men. And there's two mails a day; it comes by truck I think. And they congregate in here before and afterwards."

The post office was across the highway. Margaret Knoy once informed me on a visit there that there was no such thing as a postmistress, that she was the postmaster. I apologized and thought how easily it is to mis-address people and I was reminded of a time when I was selling cemetery lots from house to house in Philadelphia. I knocked at a nice looking row house in a middle-class neighborhood and when the door was opened by a lady I smiled and said very politely, "Is the madam in?"

She blew a fuse. I got to the edge of the porch and fled down the walk and could still hear her behind me shouting, "What kind of a neighborhood do you think you're in, Buster," and capping that with an unsavory remark rarely attributed to nice looking ladies. So I made a mental note of what Margaret told me that day; women postmasters are not *mistresses*.

When Shorty Auten's heart blew up Rev. Ramey had a special service for him at the Church of the Nazarene.

"That's right," Shorty told me. Then he laughed. "You know, I don't even go to his church."

This is pretty much the attitude of people in small towns or rural areas in southern Indiana. Everybody knows everybody and when you're sick or dying they'll all pray for you, or have a church service for you – so long as your basketball team doesn't happen to be playing their basketball team. If the latter happens to be the case then you and God are on your own. So if you're planning to get sick or start dying in one of these places during basketball season don't worry about which church you should join, just worry about which basketball team you should support.

One day during one of my first visits to Marie's she brought out a painting of a river bridge.

"This is our covered bridge at Freedom," she said, and I thought she added, "you should see it right down the road here."

I looked for that bridge for an hour and when I couldn't find it I went back to the gas station and told Marie all I could find was a steel bridge but no covered bridge.

"Well of course not," Marie said in her sweet way. "It was taken down a long time ago and moved to Indiana University. They're going to put it up there to preserve it."

It was a cold day and Marie wore a black shawl over her head and tied under her chin. A patch of gray-brown hair stuck out from under it and perched over her forehead. A waist-length quilted green jacket, brown wool skirt and nylons made up the rest of her attire.

"Isn't it cold to dress like that on this job?" I asked. "Shouldn't you wear something warmer, maybe slacks or coveralls?"

She squinched her face into a pleasant but negative reply to the first question and said in answer to the second, "I just don't wear them."

Breezy Camden was in Marie's telling about a man who was reputed to be the stingiest person in all of Freedom and Owen County, at least along the county's southern border.

"He was so tight," Breezy said from a chair, "he wouldn't give a dime to see an ant eat a bale of hay."

When I pressed for more information about him Breezy narrated the following:

178

It happened that a neighbor of the tightwad was missing firewood from his ricks on a regular basis.

"What'll I do?" he asked a friend one day. "I know it's that miser stealing from me. But I can't prove it. What'll I do?"

"I know exactly what I'd do," the man's friend said. "I'd fill a piece of firewood with black powder. I'd fix that fellow for all time."

Black powder?" the man gasped. "How would you do that?"

"Drill a hole in a piece of firewood," his friend said. "Fill the hole with black powder, seal it with mud, and put the thing back into one of the ricks."

The man who was being robbed of firewood shook his head negatively, and no more was said. A few mornings later, however, Freedom was shaken by an explosion. When residents investigated they saw black smoke billowing from the chimney atop the tightwad's house. Further investigation revealed black smoke belching out of the kitchen door. When the smoke cleared those who cared to look in the kitchen door could see the stove door lying on the floor where it had been hurled by the blast.

"That afternoon," Breezy said, "that old tightwad and his son were seen going up over the hill carrying a crosscut saw. Any firewood they burned after that was wood they cut."

"He had it coming," Marie Vest, who lounged on the Liar's Bench, said. "But if you're in honest trouble and you live in Freedom everybody here is your friend."

Mrs. Vest, who had celebrated her seventy-first birthday three days earlier, spoke from personal experience. The people of Freedom and those from the surrounding area had come to her aid after she lost her home to fire in 1971.

"Everyone helped me," she said, adjusting a red

babushka which was knotted under her chin. "I couldn't have made it without them. Yessir," she said with emphasis. "When you're in trouble, Freedom is a good place to be."

Life appeared a little brighter at Marie's one morning. The crusty, rusty gasoline pumps that had stood as weary sentinels at her filling station for so many years were gone, replaced with shiny new automatic electric reset pumps.

"Man," Marie exclaimed with a big smile, "they're like walking from the dark into daylight."

To operate them Marie needed only to pick up a nozzle and flip a switch. The act would automatically clear a computer and turn on the motor that started the pump. The pump did everything else on its own, including shutting off at the proper time. What was new about all that? Well, at Marie's in Freedom, everything. Hers was the only station in the tiny rural community at that time.

"I can't tell you how old those other pumps were because I've only been here a hundred years, myself," Marie said. She smiled at her little joke, then she added seriously, "But you held your breath when you started pumping gas."

Since my previous visit to her station Marie had suffered a bout with the flu.

"I never saw the like of it," Marie said with a frown. "All I could do was come in and sit by the stove and chill while customers took care of themselves. They made their own change from the cash drawer and did whatever needed to be done. They were just so good. I didn't lose a cent."

Wearing a beige cardigan over a red sweater over a plaid dress, and a plaid shawl around her head as guards against the cold, Marie then went out to pump gas into a pickup truck.

"Menfolks will often say to me, 'Seems like you could find an easier way to make a living,' but I tell them this isn't bad," she said on her return.

"This isn't really very hard work," she continued. "It's confining. It would be nice to take a trip, but I'm not the best traveler. If Bruce were here it might be different. He was a good guy."

They'd met at a square dance on the second floor of the old bank building at Worthington when she was a teenager, and they were married before she was twenty.

"We rented a home right here in Freedom for six dollars a month," she reminisced briefly. "Boy, it was tough to meet." She laughed girlishly.

Someone from the Liar's Bench made a comment about the new pumps, implying in jest that they should outlast her.

"They probably will," Marie smiled. "I know I'll have to quit one of these days. But I'd like to stay as long as I can."

Continuing in a serious vein, she said, "I like what I'm doing so much that if I had to do it all over again I'd be right here pumping gas."

Then as an afterthought struck her she added, "Especially now with these new pumps."

It was not long until illness overtook Marie. A cancer had invaded her body and she underwent a number of surgeries. After each one she would return to the station and tell her customers, "Well, they think they got it all this time."

"But," said a friend, "pretty soon she'd say, 'Bad news Billy, I think it's coming back,' and here she'd be in the hospital again for another operation."

Her condition deteriorated so that Marie eventually had to abandon the station, the new pumps, her customers.

"She didn't last long after she quit pumping gas," one of her customers commented.

"I had never seen her with makeup on," a lady remarked. "But at the funeral home she had on a pretty blue dress, her hair had a little curl in it, and she had a touch of makeup on her cheeks. She looked so pretty."

"It was the end of an era in Freedom when she died," said another.

Still another said, "She was so sweet. She'd put an extra twenty-five cents worth of gas in your tank."

"PICK"

Count them on your fingers as he relates them and you'll be tempted to conclude Coleman "Pick" Pickens has survived enough life threatening mishaps to make him one of the luckiest cats to have ever lived. For starters take his first basketball game as a freshman at Orleans High School against French Lick, which was played at French Lick.

Pick shot from the field three times in succession sinking the first shot and missing the next two. Lucky misses, too, for Pick was shooting at the wrong end of the court.

And his teammates Courtney Boone, John Williams, Charles Magner, George Shortridge, Howard Trinkle, Heber Brooks, Marion Cleveland and Paul Kirky, and coach Frank Kaserman, let him live.

"I was turned round," Pick explained to me many years later. "I thought that direction was east."

Four years after that, in 1931, while he was hitching a ride from Indiana Central College in Indianapolis to his home in Orleans, he encountered Earl McIntyre on a big Harley-Davidson motorcycle at Four Points.

"Tell you what, Pick," Earl suggested. "You buy me a gallon of gas and I'll give you a ride home."

"I only had fifteen cents in my pocket and I went broke right there," Pick remembered accepting the deal, "and I almost went broke for keeps in the bargain. We were just about four miles north of Orleans and Earl was going to make it as fast as he could. We were going eighty miles an hour, and him right on some guy's tail in a car. I hit him on the head, punched him on the arms, and I tried every way I knew to make him stop. If I could have just slowed him down it would have helped a little. But he wouldn't. And while we were going around a curve we hit a car head-on."

When Pick regained consciousness he was lying on a table in Dr. R. E. Baker's office in Orleans, and his left ankle was broken in four places. A promising college basketball career had suddenly come to an end.

"I landed a hundred yards down the road from the impact of that crash," Pick said. "And besides that broken ankle they picked gravel out of my head and body for hours."

Another time, minutes after Pick had installed a new mailbox in front of his house, and his neighbor had walked over and said, "My, Pick, that looks nice," and Pick had walked no more than forty feet away, a car driven by a drunk crested a rise and slammed into his mailbox at sixty miles an hour.

"He knocked that thing seventy feet into a field," Pick said. "A few seconds sooner and it would have been me, and there wouldn't have been an unbroken bone in my body."

A kidney stone attack took another of his remaining lives, and an emergency appendectomy took yet another. A variety of other attacks, including cancer of his vocal cords, combined to take some others. The last was a ruptured aneurysm.

Oddly enough not a single mishap occurred during the hours he drove a truck for the Orleans Oil Company, hours that totaled thirty-one years. Nor did any occur during the eight years he sat behind the wheel of a Lawrence County Beverage truck.

It was two years since the last threat was made on one of his remaining lives. He'd gone to the Frontier Inn "to see some of the old gang" when he was stricken.

"I wasn't sick a bit more that nothing," Pick remembered the day. "And I just fell over unconscious."

He stayed that way for ten days. In the meantime a local physician had diagnosed his problem as simply and as accurately as one might hit a nail on the head with a hammer (which probably saved the rest of Pick's lives) and he was rushed by ambulance to the Orange County Hospital in Paoli. From there he was flown by Lifeline helicopter to Jewish Hospital in Louisville, where it was learned that the aneurysm, as his doctor had suspected, had ruptured, leaving him with something less than a hope of recovery.

But like the proverbial cat with multiple lives, and to the disbelief of his doctors and his friends, Pick made it one more time. He was happy to have regained another of his many lives, but not without a touch of embarrassment. One of the volunteer EMTs on the ambulance when he was picked up at the Frontier Inn the day he was stricken was Pick's minister, Ralph Austin, pastor of the Old Union Methodist Church. But Pick managed to live through that too.

"I just don't know how many close calls I've had," Pick said with a hand pressed to his head for emphasis. "After all that's happened to me I'm lucky to be alive after seventy-five years."

After hearing those words some of his old friends who were gathered around listening to all of this voted by acclamation to give him a total of ninety-nine years to live out however many lives he may have had left to him.

To which Pick replied, "No sir. I'm going to live to a hundred, or die trying."

He very nearly did in the strangest of accidents. He fell out of the shower in his own house. A tall bag of bones like Pick must have made a gosh-awful racket when he did, and it nearly scared his wife, Margie, to death. She ran to the bathroom to find Pick wrapped in the shower curtain and sprawled all over the place with his head hanging over the toilet.

"Did you hurt yourself," Margie cried, thinking that her husband had broken his head and maybe every bone in his long, lanky body, and that she probably should have been calling 911 instead of asking him silly questions.

"I don't know," Pick gasped, the breath just about knocked out of him. "But for God's sake," he continued hurriedly, "don't flush the toilet."

The basketball game against French Lick was in 1927. In spite of Pick's confusion Orleans went on to win that night. And Pick himself went on to be some kind of basketball player. He had ability and height, sometimes more of the latter than he thought. Howard Trinkle said Pick was tall enough in those days to scratch an elbow on the rim of a basket in one game.

"He just jumped high enough to do that, and that was pretty tall," Howard said.

How tall was that? Well, Pick was in the country store at Valeen one day and a little old lady customer looked up into his face and called out, "How tall are you, sonny?"

Pick replied, "Five-feet-eighteen."

The little old lady leaned precariously backwards and took another look up at him. "Aw!" she exclaimed, obviously misunderstanding what he'd said. "You're taller than that."

In those days six-feet-six set a basketball player apart, and Pick might have gone on to greater things had he not had fifteen cents in his pocket that fateful day Earl had come along on his big hog. But, as time proved, that wasn't the first nor the last time a ball had taken a bad bounce for Pick. No one was more aware of that than his physician.

"'You've had just about everything happen to you, haven't you Pick,'" Pick quoted him as saying one day.

And without a moment's hesitation Pick replied, "Yep. One miscarriage would make it about everything."

RIP
OF RIP, VAN & WINKLE

We were six miles west of Medora, six miles southwest of Leesville, and three miles northeast of Fort Ritner, standing at the back side of a sandy patch that was his summer garden. Mary Lee had sent me to him.

"He knows all about Sparksville," she assured me from the porch of her white frame house. Mary Lee was a lady of small stature with hair the color of her house. "He can tell you all you want to know," she said.

All I wanted to know? All I wanted to know was why the town was there, so alone, so – quiet? Not exactly, maybe. Leesville and Fort Ritner were alone and quiet. So were Solsberry, Koleen, and Cuba, not to mention Newark, and Bartlettsville. Maybe I really didn't want to know anything in particular about the place. Free to make the choice as I was, I might have passed up his house had he not been standing at the back side of his garden.

We waved and "helloed" and met in the middle of what turned out to be a sandy patch of growing things. He had planted beans, tomatoes, corn – all those things that people plant in a vegetable garden. A large section was given to strawberry bushes from which hung an abundance of fruit still too green for eating.

"Too bad you didn't wait and come a week later," he smiled an old smile. "I'd of given you a quart of them to take home."

I made a hurried promise to return, and he smiled again, wiping the palm of a large hand across his mouth and chin.

"Oh, hell yes," he exclaimed with restrained enthusiasm in answer to my first question about Sparksville. "We had everything here at one time. There was a sawmill, a flour mill, four stores. I'll say, we had everything here. Jim Star had a store, and Ed McPike, and the Lewis brothers. And Frank Mullin had a saloon right there." He pointed down the hill from the garden patch.

"Of course, we had the railroad; the B & O. We had some high old times in this town. And them wops from Sicily came in to work for the railroad and, boy, they were the best musicians you ever heard. There were a couple of hotels: Kate Lee ran one, and Frank Mullin's wife ran the other. Dan Hunsucker had the livery, and seven trains a day stopped here. I'll bet we had a population of four hundred.

"Let me tell you something," he ran his hand over his mouth and chin again. His blue eyes under the green brim of his Nutrena Feeds cap were wide, clear, honest. "See that old church there? See them hills all around here?"

He had pointed, then he waved an arm in the direction of the tree covered hills that rose green and high around us.

"Used to when they rang the bell in that church, the people would come out of those hills. My goodness! You never saw the like! Why they'd come down in buggies and on horseback. The people in the town would

189

join them at church. Well, I'll tell you, there were so many people you couldn't get around. There was standing room only at the church."

The account had been something of an exertion. He stood quietly, nodding his head in solemn affirmation of what he had said, and, no doubt, of what he hadn't said but which then must have been passing in colorful pageant behind those blue eyes.

"I was born here in 1902," he resumed. "When I was sixteen I went to work for the railroad for sixteen and a half cents an hour for a ten-hour day. When the first world's war came along I went into the Army and they put me in the 20th U.S. Infantry and sent me down to the Mexican border.

"When it was over I went back to work for the B & O, and I stayed there until I retired. I was in maintenance. I'd catch No. 55 and go clean to Montgomery, Indiana, to work; and I'd get back here at nine o'clock at night. That was something, I'll tell you."

He turned and faced downhill from his garden patch. From under the bill of his cap, his blue eyes studied the flatland there, a long line of trees that grew thick there. He said they marked the "river." The East Fork of White River.

Only that morning a neighbor had caught fifty pounds of catfish – huge delicious catfish – while fishing in its waters. He smiled at the memory. He savored it. Still smiling, he said that he had lived his whole life in Sparksville and that he and his wife, Nellie, reared a family of seven children there. He said he stayed in the town because he got so poor that he could get no further. But there was a euphoric lilt to his words when he spoke of one of his twin sons, now dead.

"He and his brother were in the Korean war; all through it," he said of the dead twin. "Believe me.

When they came home I said, 'Why don't you get out of here and go someplace where there's something to do.' And he said to me, 'Dad, if you went through what I went through, you'd know why I don't. I just love this old sand.' That's what he said."

We looked down at the sand under our shoes. He pushed a small ridge together with the toe of a big shoe. He nodded his head again.

"We've got one mile square of sand land here," he said.

He raised a hand and pointed first in one direction and then another until he had outlined it in the distance, until he explained the location of its four borders.

"I don't know why we've got it," he continued. "We've just got it. I call it rabbit sand; I've got my garden in rabbit sand. Hard to grow anything in it. I'm going to quit it. This is going to be my last year." He looked squarely at me. "Maybe this will be *my* last year."

It was difficult to ignore those words. But I looked at the six-feet-two of him, the ample girth of him, and I disagreed with him, and I told him so. He was unimpressed.

"I don't know what you'd call this place," he again turned to view the area surrounded by the green hills; Sparksville. "I just call it a holler. That creek over yonder, they call that Fountainhead Holler Creek; comes from up there." He pointed. "There are some springs up there – I guess you'd call them Fountainhead Holler Springs – and they never go dry. Nope. I don't know what you'd call it, I guess.

"When I was a kid," he directed his words along the route of another memory, "people here were more sociable, and they liked to help one another. Now it seems that they are indifferent. And they have differ-

191

ent churches now. I don't know if that's good. Maybe. Maybe not.

"When I was a kid, this is where I went to school," he continued. "Nellie went to school here, too. That's all changed."

His blue eyes lit up briefly at another recollection.

"One time when they were reading the story of Rip Van Winkle in school, three of us fell asleep. From that day on they called the three of us by nicknames; one was Rip, one was Van, and the other was Winkle. All our lives we went by those names."

He laughed slowly, pleasantly, and he placed his right palm flat to his waist as though he were really enjoying himself. Then he looked squarely at me again.

"I'm the one that was named Rip," he said with a broad smile. "That's what they call me around here – Rip. But my real name is Raymond. Raymond Huffman."

THE REVENOOER

Counting the elderly and the little children, there were about three hundred people in the small hill town, so anything out of the ordinary became quickly apparent. That's how come Granny Tredwit was so quick to spot the revenue agent.

She was related to almost everybody in town, and everybody in town knew that Granny secretly distilled and illegally sold what she called white mule. "Nothin's got a kick quite like it," she used to say. "That's why I call it white mule."

Like most other women in town Granny was a church-goer. She also belonged to the ladies aid. Long-widowed, and too proud to accept handouts from the township trustee, she felt she should make her own living. If she chose to secretly distill white mule in the old shed behind her house in order to do so, no one faulted her for that. Especially those people she called her "clients."

When one of her grandsons got old enough to dare question her about the morality of making moonshine he said, "Granny, they taught us in Sunday School that it was a sin to drink whiskey."

"Only if you buy it in a store, son. Only if you buy it in a store," Granny replied testily. "I make mine from God-grown ingredients only. Ain't no sin to consume God's own handiwork."

She got no argument about that. But Granny all the

same was always nervously on the alert for strangers in town. "He just could be a revenooer," she used to say when she spotted one.

It might have been a salesman at the village store, or just anyone, for that matter, she was that suspicious of everyone. That's how she was able one day to spot a revenooer so quickly. And she wasted no time getting on the telephone to one of her several grandchildren who lived in town.

"Julie," she whispered hoarsely into the phone when her granddaughter answered. "Bring your shotgun quick. I've got a problem down here."

She'd had a problem once before and had summoned Julie and her shotgun to help solve it. Granny had wanted to dispense with a strange varmint that was hidden in her gooseberry bush.

"Come quick," she had shouted to Julie over the phone that day. "I'll get the hoe and you bring your shotgun and we'll kill the devilish thing."

Julie, who had hunted squirrels and rabbits all her life and was reputed to be one of the best shots in the county, grabbed her 12-gauge, open-choke shotgun and rushed down to Granny's. Sure enough, there in the gooseberry bush, almost hidden by lush green leaves and thumb-size radiant green fruit, was the varmint. Without hesitation Julie pulled up and let go a shot. BLAM!

The thing went straight up, hit a snarl of branches of the gooseberry bush, and flopped out almost at the women's feet. Granny screamed and raised the hoe and struck it a blow. The thing bounced up and when it hit the ground again it was near Julie's feet. She let out a loud squawk and backed up as though she would let go another shot at it. But each time Granny struck it with the hoe the thing would spring right back up toward the two women.

"Stand back, I'll shoot it again," Julie would shout.

"I'll have one more lick," Granny would call back and she'd wallop the thing with the hoe again.

And that's the way it went for a while, Granny, her skirts flying, jumping and shouting and striking that thing with the hoe, and Julie, her skirts also flying, dancing around pointing the shotgun, shouting for a clear shot at it. It was a sight to see and hear. Finally, through their combined efforts and antics, the thing lay unmoving in the dust. They were sure that whatever it was they had succeeded in killing it.

"What is it?" Granny asked, not sure she wanted to get too close to the thing.

"I don't know," her granddaughter replied.

"Maybe you had better take another shot at it," Granny suggested. "Make certain it's dead."

"It's probably dead all right," said Julie with relief. "It's not moving."

Only after they were absolutely sure it was dead did they venture close enough to identify it – a large, colorful, rubber alligator toy that belonged to one of Julie's nephews, Granny's great grandson.

"We had no gooseberry pie that year," the great-grandson later remembered the mess his aunt Julie's shot had made of the gooseberry bush.

So in this latest episode, when Julie arrived at Granny's with her shotgun she expected to find another beast to shoot. Wrong. This time Granny had discovered a revenue agent.

"I saw him agoin' from house t'house," she said excitedly to Julie. "Just apokin' around. I know he's alookin' for my still. Just you put a shot over his head and scare him out of town."

Granny was right. There was a man going from yard to yard, poking around. Julie studied him for a while and then turned to Granny. "That ain't no revenooer, Granny," she said. "That's only the electric company meter reader."

195

BLIND HORSE ROAD

The foxes were so hard on the chickens they roosted in trees, and the old rooster sounded like the clack valve in his crowing system might have dropped prematurely, but life on Blind Horse Road was still about as good as it ever was, and better than in most places.

Every Fourth of July the Hanners came home to Eldon Hanner's house. They'd roll out a flat-bed farm wagon, open some folding tables, get some folding chairs from the school, and have probably the biggest family reunion around.

A hundred or more souls gathered in Eldon's yard, all Hanners, or with Hanner blood lines, and in-laws, and prepared enough food for a log-rolling. Then they sat around and ate it, and talked about old times on Blind Horse Road, on the banks of Blind Horse Creek.

"The little ones played in the stream, or in the fields," said Eldon as though he were savoring again the pleasure of it all as he leaned on a fence post. "My brothers and sisters usually visited 'Old Place Holler,' the cabin is still there, and they'd even take their food up there to eat, and talk about when we was kids."

Eldon was born in a log house which still stood on Blind Horse Road, as were two other Hanner children. Eight others were born in another log house which was situated about a quarter mile west of Eldon's place, in a hollow known as Old Place Holler.

196

The Hanners were the children of the late Ralph and Kimmie Sarah Bowman Hanner. The old log school and the old church they attended as children still stood on Eldon's place and, in their time, those aging edifices were known as Blind Horse School and Blind Horse Church.

"The name, as I always heard it," Eldon shifted elbows on the top of the fence post as he answered my query, "come from old Mart Henry's blind horse falling off a bluff up north there and killing hisself."

The epitaph had been preserved. About a mile south of Eldon's place, where the road forked and one gravelly tine climbed a sloping hogback to Gorbett's Chapel and the other wound its smooth blacktop surface to cousin Joe Hanner's place where it dead-ended north of Eldon's, there was a green and white Jackson County road sign memorializing Mart Henry's dead horse.

"Blind Horse Road," it read, pointing in the direction of the Hanners' properties. The Hanners also had committed themselves to preserving the name.

Possum and dressing, sweet potatoes, groundhog, rabbit, and squirrel, and squirrel and dumplings, were hardy and frequent fare when the Hanners were growing up, but Eldon observed, "I ain't eat a possum in years."

A tall man, and hefty around, Eldon wore bib overalls, a blue chambray shirt, and a black-billed summer cap that shaded his blue eyes. He took it off once and ran his hand over his head.

"Oh," he said reminiscing, "I worked in a factory one time as a young man, but I couldn't get my heart into it, and I come back here."

As a young man – as young people – Eldon and the Hanners walked into the railhead at Kurtz a couple of miles south of their home. They played a lot of base-

197

ball then, and at least twice a year Kurtz and the surrounding area hosted a medicine show. Eldon remembered that Ruth Marshall, her sister Frieda Marshall Noe, who lived over around Houston, Jim Conner, and Charles Fleetwood were his teachers in the old school. It was closed about fifty years earlier and had since become a part of Eldon's barn and could be seen from Blind Horse Road.

Seven children were born in Eldon's house, and they went on to have nine children. Three smaller ones of the latter offspring were on the banks of Blind Horse Creek, one with a makeshift fishing pole with a long string that hung down into the water.

"I don't have no bait on it," he smiled at us.

Across Blind Horse Road and Blind Horse Creek, about a mile up the hollow east of Eldon's house, Gorbett's Baptist Chapel sat quietly in the intersection of Gorbett's Chapel Road and Houston Road. Eldon recalled walking up the hollow numerous times to attend services there.

Eldon owned nearly three hundred and fifty acres of land, about a hundred twenty-five of which were tillable. He ran about a hundred head of cattle and about a hundred and fifty hogs on the rest of it, except that part which was in timber. He'd lived there all his life, and found it peaceful, the people congenial and themselves.

Although the foxes worried the chickens into the trees, and the old rooster's cockadoodledoo wasn't up to par, the hens managed to lay enough eggs for the Hanners' own use. And that wasn't bad.

It was in 1931 that Delight arrived at Blind Horse Road. Her trip there began about 1929, when Delight was a sophomore at Houston School. Joe Hanner and his brother Merritt used to make the four or five mile trip there from their home to provide music between the acts of school plays. Joe played the fiddle and Merritt played the guitar.

Delight, a sophomore when she first saw Joe, fell in love with him. This was just one of those sitting and looking kind of romances, not one of those hand-holding things.

"Oh, no," Delight remembered. "They wouldn't allow anything like that in school." From just sitting and looking, Delight concluded that Joe Hanner "was just a right guy, so easy-talking, and easy-going." All the time, too, she was plotting Joe's end of freedom, and how she was going to one day make it to Blind Horse Road.

The sitting and looking went on during the remainder of her school years. With one difference. Joe had become interested enough to be paying her occasional social calls at her sister's house in Houston; Mrs. Floyd Hendricks' house.

Delight's parents, Mr. and Mrs. Hezekiah "Kite" Axsom lived in Brown County, just east of the Monroe County line, near the Deckard Cemetery, where Delight had grown up. Because there was no high school there for her to attend she stayed at her sister's and attended the old white frame that was Houston School.

Then it happened. Joe helped Delight up on the running board of his cigar box-like Essex one day, and seated her inside the pretentiously upholstered coupe. And he packed her off to Bloomington and the courthouse there. They obtained a marriage license and, while still in the courthouse, they walked into the office of a justice of the peace who was a friend to Kite Axsom, and he married them.

And Delight went from there to the fork in the road that leads into Blind Horse Road. She rode under trees, tall and rustling, where the sun shone down on green pastures. She passed towering sunflowers that drooped wearily under their fruitful burdens. And finally she arrived at a white frame that sat appealingly on a high knoll surrounded by giant oak and maple trees that spread their massive tops to cool it in the summer.

From a porch across the front of their house Blind Horse Road, the land, the trees, the sky, the world, could be seen with unworried ease. And from a limb of one of the giant trees, a swing – the old fashioned kind in which a child could swing as high as the sky – was suspended. There she and Joe lived happily ever after.

Delight was a pretty lady, and a gracious hostess. It was small wonder to me that Joe hadn't brought her to Blind Horse Road sooner than he did. At seventy-two Joe continued working their farm, including, on a hot day, cutting and putting up hay.

There were other Hanners on Blind Horse Road besides Eldon, Merritt, and Joe; Philip and Woodrow. And quite often people who visited would ask, "Why don't you call this place Hannertown?"

Delight would laugh at the suggestion, and maybe it is well she did, and that the Hanners didn't name their unblemished niche in the world Hannertown. There wouldn't have been a Blind Horse Road for her to have come to November 15, 1931.

For more than fifty years Joe took time from farming to cut hair on Saturdays and on Wednesday evenings in a small shop on State Road 58 at Kurtz. It had an eye-catching Wildroot hair tonic sign out front. I used to wonder when I passed it after my visit with the Hanners if Joe ever related to any of his customers the story of Delight's trip from Houston School to Blind Horse Road, and of the friendly, gentle people who lived there.

THE MOUSE THAT CAME IN FROM THE COLD

If you live near the house where this reportedly happened one night you probably already know the story. But I'll go ahead and tell it anyway for those who haven't yet heard it. If I should make a mistake or two please forgive me. After all, I wasn't there. All I know is what I've been told.

As it was recounted to me, the story begins with the end of balmy weather and the first nocturnal temperature plunge into the twenties. Fearing for the safety of the plants she had on the porch, a worried housewife brought them inside.

Hurried and anxious as she was she failed to notice a shivering tiny mouse that was feasting on the roots of one of the plants. He also wasn't aware of being carried inside until he felt the welcome warmth.

It was an unusual treat for the little creature and in his joy he forgot his hunger and his manners. He jumped out of the plant pot and began doing happy handsprings on the living room carpet.

Seeing him the housewife let out a scream that could be heard a country mile away and she jumped up on a chair where she screamed some more.

Hearing all the noise the poor little mouse was terror stricken, and he dashed across the floor and took refuge under the couch. Feeling relatively safe, he crouched there, every so often peeping pop-eyed at the woman standing on the chair who was screaming at the top of her lungs.

In the upstairs bathroom at this time the woman's husband was taking a shower. Above the sound of the splashing water he heard his wife's screams. Gripped by the fear that some terrible accident had suddenly befallen her, he flung open the shower door, plunged out of the bathroom, pounded down the stairs, and skidded into the living room as naked as a jaybird and dripping like a wet dish rag.

Shouting to be heard over his wife's screams he asked what she was doing on the chair screaming like she was.

Holding her skirt above her knees with one hand she pointed to the couch with the other and wailed that she had been attacked by a big rat then hiding under the couch, and that he should kill it.

By this time the neighbors had become aware that something unusual was happening and they had come to their doors and windows to better listen.

In the meantime the protective, dutiful husband got down on his hands and knees and began looking under the couch for the big rat that had invaded his home and attacked his wife. While she was screaming from the chair that he should watch out and be careful he saw the vicious animal.

The little mouse, its tiny heart pounding like a jackhammer, lay cringing in fear and wondering what in the world all the commotion was about.

Feeling threatened by what he saw under the couch, the husband jumped up and ran to the utility closet and availed himself of the household broom. Back in the living room he got down on his hands and knees again and began poking under the couch with it.

Seeing that he was in danger of being mauled, maybe even squished to death by the poking broom, the little mouse began taking evasive action. When the husband poked in one direction the little mouse dodged in the opposite direction. And so the whacky contest continued.

The resultant racket was incredible. So awful was it that it awakened the family collie sleeping in front of a hot air wall register in the kitchen. He got up, stretched, and moseyed into the living room. There he was stopped dead in his tracks. He had lived in the house for many years and had never witnessed a scene such as that he now beheld.

His mistress was standing on a chair holding her skirt above her knees with one hand and gesticulating with the other while a naked man was on his hands and knees on the floor hollering and poking a broom under the couch.

Swelling with curiosity the big dog stealthily approached the naked man. He thought it was his master, but because he had never seen him naked and in that position before he couldn't be certain. So he resorted to the one sure method dogs have of identification. He stuck his cold nose to the husband's bare backside and took a big sniff.

The husband reacted as though he'd been stuck with a high voltage rod for he let out a piercing scream, the loudest the neighbors had heard that night.

Then he zoomed right up almost to the ceiling and flopped down on his back in a dead faint.

That's when the neighbors called 911.

When the ambulance arrived the crew lifted the naked husband off the floor, placed him on a stretcher, covered him with a blanket, and started out the door.

That was just what the little mouse had been waiting for, someone to open a door and let him out of that looney bin.

He darted out from under the couch, headed for the open door, getting there at the same time as the guys carrying the stretcher.

Seeing the little mouse charging toward them like that, one of the men screamed, let go his end of the stretcher dumping the husband on the floor, and joined the screaming housewife on the chair.

It wasn't easy, for the dog had got there ahead of him and there was very little room left.

When they finally got the husband to the hospital they had a heck of a time trying to explain to the emergency room nurse how he broke his arm.

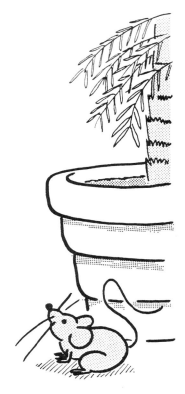

THE TIN CAN MAN

To order extra copies of Larry Incollingo's books please fill out the coupon below and mail to:

Reunion Books
3949 Old SR446
Bloomington, IN 47401
Or Call 812-336-8403

For multiple order special discount (three or more books) call 812-336-8403.

Please send me:

_____ copies of *The Tin Can Man* @ $10.50 each.

_____ copies of *ECHOES of Journeys Past* @ $10.50 each.

_____ copies of *Ol' Sam Payton* @ $9.50 each.

_____ copies of *Precious Rascal* @ $9.50 each.

_____ copies of *G'bye My Honey* @ $9.50 each.

_____ copies of *Laughing All The Way* @ $9.50 each.

Add 5% Sales Tax, Plus $2.00 M& H (up to 3 books).

NAME: _____

ADDRESS:_____

CITY, STATE, ZIP: _____

TELEPHONE: _____

SEND A GIFT COPY TO A FRIEND